E

"I think it's good for Spike to be around a man."

"It's good for me to be around him, too. Not that I'm in any hurry, but I'm looking forward to having children of my own someday. I think I'll have a lot to give them."

Jill's chest tightened until she could hardly breathe. This man, who had so many of the qualities she'd nearly despaired of finding, wanted the one thing in life she couldn't give him.

Children.

"Thanks for reading to him," she managed to say before the silence lengthened awkwardly.

"I'll look forward to seeing you at the housewarming tomorrow." Chad lingered near the front door, studying her.

"I'm not sure…"

"Three o'clock," he said, and went out the door before she could refuse.

Dear Reader,

Harlequin American Romance is celebrating the holidays with four wonderful books for you to treasure all season long, starting with the latest installment in the RETURN TO TYLER series. Bestselling author Judy Christenberry charms us with her delightful story of a sought-after bachelor who finds himself falling for a single mother and longing to become part of her *Patchwork Family*.

In Pamela Browning's *Baby Christmas*, soon after a department store Santa urges a lovely woman to make a wish on Christmas Eve, she finds a baby on her doorstep and meets a handsome handyman. To win custody of her nephew, a loving aunt decides her only resource is to pretend to be engaged to a *Daddy, M.D.* Don't miss this engaging story from Jacqueline Diamond.

Rounding out the month is Harlequin American Romance's innovative story, *Twin Expectations* by Kara Lennox. In this engaging volume, identical twin sisters pledge to become mothers—with or without husbands—by their thirtieth birthday. As the baby hunt heats up, the sisters unexpectedly find love with two gorgeous half brothers.

Next month, look for Harlequin American Romance's spin-off of TEXAS CONFIDENTIAL, Harlequin Intrigue's in-line continuity series, and another WHO'S THE DADDY? title from Muriel Jensen.

I hope you enjoy all our romance novels this month. All of us at Harlequin Books wish you a wonderful holiday season!

Melissa Jeglinski
Associate Senior Editor
Harlequin American Romance

DADDY, M.D.
Jacqueline Diamond

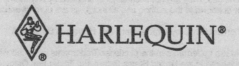

HARLEQUIN®

TORONTO • NEW YORK • LONDON
AMSTERDAM • PARIS • SYDNEY • HAMBURG
STOCKHOLM • ATHENS • TOKYO • MILAN • MADRID
PRAGUE • WARSAW • BUDAPEST • AUCKLAND

Special thanks to Anna M. Cotter
and the Brea Mall

ISBN 0-373-16855-1

DADDY, M.D.

Copyright © 2000 by Jackie Hyman.

ABOUT THE AUTHOR

Writing about doctors comes naturally to Jacqueline Diamond. Her father was a country doctor in Menard, Texas, before becoming a psychiatrist and practicing in Louisville, Kentucky, and Nashville, Tennessee. She also has two sons who make their share of visits to the pediatrician.

Jackie currently lives in Southern California. You can reach her at P.O. Box 1315, Brea, CA 92822.

Books by Jacqueline Diamond

HARLEQUIN AMERICAN ROMANCE

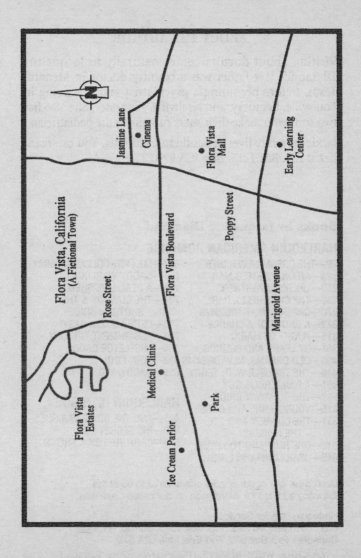

Flora Vista, California
(A Fictional Town)

Chapter One

"Doctor, we have a little boy here who says he lost his tonsils. And I think he's lost his mother, too."

Chad Markham didn't immediately react to the receptionist's comments. Instead he finished making notes on the chart of the little girl he'd just examined. He didn't want to forget that the medication that had cured her ear infection had also given her a slight rash.

Handing the chart to his efficient nurse as she breezed past in the corridor, he turned his attention to the receptionist. In her early twenties, Susie Nunez was bouncy and breathless and fell in love with every child and half the doctors at the clinic.

Right now she was gazing at Chad dewy-eyed. "The kid's adorable!" she said. "He looks like Count Dracula."

Chad tried, and failed, to imagine a little boy, adorable or otherwise, who resembled a vampire. "Long teeth?" he guessed.

"No! It's his hair," Susie said. "Maybe it's a dye job from Halloween. I don't know."

"And he has what kind of medical complaint?" Instinctively Chad glanced at his watch.

Doctors were always running behind schedule, and

today was no exception. Now that his 7 a.m. to 4 p.m. shift was over, half an hour late, he faced several pressing matters. Two of them were likely to chew up his patio furniture if they didn't get fed.

"Tonsils," Susie repeated. "He says he lost them. He wants to see a doctor right away. He's a very determined little boy."

"You say he's unaccompanied?" he queried.

Susie nodded.

"How old?"

"About five," she said.

It was Friday, and Chad was more than ready to make the switch from hardworking doctor to weekend fun-seeking bachelor. Despite his eagerness to shed his responsibilities, however, he needed to attend to this little boy. He was either lost or a runaway, and Chad never turned his back on a youngster in need.

"Bring him into my office, would you?" As the receptionist hurried away, he retreated to his book-crammed cubicle at the end of the hall.

From a drawer he retrieved a box of sugar-free lollipops. Treats had worked wonders in getting kids to talk during the three years he'd spent at an inner-city hospital in Los Angeles. This past year, since he'd come to the Flora Vista Medical Clinic in a comfortable southern California suburb, he'd found that middle-class kids weren't much different at heart.

Footsteps approached along the hall. Chad looked up as Susie appeared in the doorway, escorting a slender tyke with earnest brown eyes.

The most striking thing about him was his jet-black hair, crested by a widow's peak. Although Halloween was only two weeks past, Chad doubted anyone had dyed the boy's hair for the occasion.

"Hello, there," he told the youngster.

"This is Dr. Markham," Susie explained.

"Hi." With no sign of shyness, the five-year-old planted himself in the doorway. He wore faded jeans, a T-shirt and a denim jacket with a brownish stain on the front. "I'm Spike."

It was hard not to chuckle at the nickname. But kids hated to be laughed at. "You can call me Chad," he said with a straight face. "Now, what's this about your tonsils?"

"They're gone," the little boy announced.

"They vanished? Presto magico?"

"Well, not exactly. I mean, they hurt. Kind of," Spike said unconvincingly.

What was he dealing with here? Chad wondered. A sick boy who needed treatment, or a lonely kid seeking attention? "How long have they been hurting?"

"A few days." Spike thought over his statement before adding, "Then they fell out."

From behind him, Susie put in, "Tonsils don't fall out."

"Mine did," the boy said calmly. "Now I need ice cream."

The truth dawned. This child was neither ill nor abandoned. He was a clever rogue trying to scam his favorite dessert.

Perhaps he lived in one of the houses on the streets behind the clinic. Although Chad didn't approve of letting children this young run around unsupervised, he knew that some parents allowed it.

"Let me guess," he said. "A while ago you had your tonsils removed and were given lots of ice cream, right?"

His dark hair bobbed as Spike nodded. "And now I lost them again."

"You can't lose your tonsils," Susie said. "Anyway, once they're gone, that's it. You can't grow more."

"Are you a doctor?" Spike asked.

"No..."

"A nurse?"

"No, but..."

The boy drew himself up to his full height, which was maybe three feet. "I think we should leave this to the medical exp-expect..."

"Experts," Chad finished.

"That's it," the kid said.

One couldn't help admiring the boy's nerve, and his vocabulary, too. Anyway, Chad was off duty now, and *somebody* needed to take Spike home.

"I'll tell you what," he said. "I'll walk you over to the Frosty Shoppe next door and buy you a cone. But only if you promise to show me where you live."

Spike bit his lip before replying. "I'm not sure I can find it."

"Why not?"

"I've only lived there a month," he said.

"You and your parents?"

"I don't have any parents."

During his inner-city years, Chad had met a lot of foster children, and this little charmer sounded as if he might be one. If so, the doctor would have a few sharp words for the caretaker who allowed him to wander around so freely.

"Don't worry. I'll help you get home." After shrugging off his white coat, he was ready. "Let's go, sport. I mean, Spike."

AS SHE DROVE HOME past the Flora Vista Medical Clinic, Jill Rutledge was furious about Santa Claus.

She didn't care how tall he was. Or how fat. Or even whether his whiskers ran a bit on the scraggly side. And a magical old elf could certainly belong to any racial or ethnic group, or all of them combined.

One thing she did know about Santa, though. There was only one of him.

One at a time, anyway.

She'd been stewing ever since this afternoon when her boss announced that this year the mall of Flora Vista was going to spread its umbrella wider than ever by offering a choice of St. Nicks. This year children could opt for the ethnicity of their choice, or they could visit all five Santas. Side by side.

"And of course we'll be having Mrs. Claus again," Bertrand Larkin, the marketing director, had added with a smile at Jill across the conference table. "Actually, it was your excellent suggestion last year that inspired me to expand our Santa base."

"But, Bert," she'd said, ignoring the approving nods of the half dozen other staff members, "adding Mrs. Claus didn't violate the integrity of the Santa legend."

"We're not violating it, we're improving it!" crowed Bert, a thin, birdlike man with a distracted air. "It's the latest trend, to be inclusive!"

In the five years that she'd worked in marketing for the mall, Jill had discovered that her boss had a genius for detecting the prevailing winds and bending with them. She'd never met anyone so stubborn in his wishy-washiness.

Even so, she was about to protest this flagrant disrespect for tradition, when the mall's general manager, Delores Hadley, spoke up. "Excellent idea, Bert," she'd said. "We might even get some good press out of this."

Frowning with frustration at the memory, Jill drove through the gate of the Terrace Crest Estates. These weren't really estates, just single-family homes on slightly larger-than-average lots.

Her tension eased as she drove along the meandering streets between earth-toned houses with well-tended landscaping. She'd bought a home here after her divorce and had filled the airy rooms with pastel colors, smothered the yard in flowers and created a loving home for her two cats.

When she reached her driveway, Jill clicked open the garage door and pulled inside. Gardening tools hung neatly on pegs. Storage boxes sat, clearly labeled, on shelves at the back. Everything in its place.

It was nearly four-thirty, she saw by the car's clock. By five-fifteen she needed to reclaim her nephew from her next-door neighbor, but since she was allowed to leave early on Fridays, she had a few minutes to get settled.

Collecting her briefcase, Jill let herself into the house. The air still smelled of rye toast from breakfast, honey from the bran muffins she'd baked last night and the tiniest trace of *odeur de kitty*.

"Hi, Normal," she told the ginger cat snoozing on the sofa in the living room. "Where's Neurotic?"

The cat uttered a soft greeting and regarded her hopefully. The housebound male had been known to shift position as much as four inches to get a massage, but that was the extent of his tricks.

Her other cat, a stray who had moved into her yard and never left, was another story. Neurotic refused to stay in one place for more than half an hour, and came indoors only for short periods.

Jill had tried locking her in, but she'd somehow learned to turn a doorknob. After arriving home twice to find the side door ajar, she'd yielded to the inevitable and installed a pet door.

Striding through the rooms, Jill deposited her briefcase on the glass table in the den. Pulling out a brush, she ran it through her frazzled silver-blonde hair. By this hour on a Friday she was ready to wilt.

A blur of movement in the rear yard caught her eye. Jill unlocked the French doors to the patio. "Neurotic?" she called, and halted in shock.

Her exquisite backyard lay in tatters. Clumps of grass had been torn up. Flowers lay with their roots exposed. Even the rose trellis stood askew.

On a rise at the back of the yard a shaggy Irish setter raised its head and barked. A black spaniel peered through an open wrought iron gate in the rear fence and added its voice to the cacophony.

Who on earth had taken the padlock off the gate? A previous owner of Jill's house, whose sister had occupied the house directly behind, had installed the opening for convenience, but subsequent owners had kept it secured by mutual consent.

"Get out!" Jill could feel her temper rising. "Out! Out!" Without pausing to consider that the dogs might bite, she rushed toward the rear of the yard, and they fled uphill through the gate.

Furious, she jammed it shut, found the open lock lying on the ground and snapped it into place. The house behind hers had gone into escrow two months ago, and she'd seen painters sprucing up the exterior the previous week, but this was the first sign that anyone had moved in. It wasn't a good omen for her relationship with her new neighbors, Jill reflected, brushing a couple of leaves from her light wool suit.

She was about to resume calling her cat, when, at the house to her right, the patio door opened and Yvette O'Reilly came out. "Oh, Jill!" Her neighbor's hands fluttered. "Thank goodness you're home."

Yvette, a seventy-three-year-old retired office manager, had been baby-sitting Jill's nephew for the past month. Jill's heart sank. Troubles always came in threes, so she was due for one more blow. "Is Spike all right?"

"I can't find him!" The cherubic woman's eyes brimmed with tears. "One minute he was watching TV and now—well, he isn't anywhere."

Jill forgot her irritation with whoever had moved into the house behind hers. "Are you sure he isn't in the bathroom? Or out here, exploring?"

Her neighbor's yard, which was separated from hers by a four-foot wall, contained more than its share of lures for a child. These included a gazebo, a chipped birdbath, pink lawn flamingos, a partially constructed latticework shade house on the slope, and an oversize doghouse that hadn't been used since before Jill had moved next door.

"I shouted 'Ice cream!' If he'd heard me, he would have broken his neck getting to the kitchen," said her neighbor. "You know how he feels about ice cream."

"I do." Jill, who watched her diet strictly, had been hoping to get her new ward hooked on frozen yogurt instead. So far it hadn't worked. "How long has he been missing?"

"About half an hour," Yvette admitted. "I walked up and down the block, and then I thought I'd check in case he came back while I was gone. He isn't over at your house by any chance?''

"No." Still, although Spike couldn't have climbed the wall, he was bold enough to have gone out Yvette's front door and entered Jill's yard through the side gate, seeking an open door.

Her doors were locked. But the open rear gate might have tempted the curious little boy. "I'll check the yard behind me."

"Do you want me to call the police?"

What would a real parent do in this situation? Jill wondered. She had no idea. For a woman who had no trouble coping with the business world, she felt inadequate when it came to children. She hadn't planned to adopt one. In fact, she'd resigned herself to never having any.

She did know one thing, though: calling the police meant filing a report. That might complicate the adoption procedure and create bureaucratic hassles.

"Let me look around first," she said. "He's probably gone exploring and made a new friend. If he turns up, please call me on my cell phone."

Yvette nodded eagerly. "Of course. I'm so sorry."

Jill wanted to reassure her but couldn't find the words or spare the time. Instead she rushed to the rear gate, unlocked it and went through.

The lot behind hers sat on a flat terrace, its view of her property broken only by a vine-covered fence. When she entered the yard, the two dogs looked up and wagged their tails, but neither barked.

"Spike?" she called, stepping across the yard. Her medium-heeled pumps sank into the soft ground, and at any moment she expected an irate homeowner to come storming out and confront her.

Whoever had moved in here must be planning to host some parties. There was a large barbecue grill and an array of new patio furniture, including half a dozen lounge chairs. From the whirlpool bath, which had been empty the last time she'd peeked over the fence, steam rose into the November air.

For an alarmed moment Jill feared her nephew might have gone into the water, but a closer inspection of the tiled pool showed it to be empty. Nevertheless, she felt even angrier at whoever had opened the gate between their yards, for exposing a child to danger.

Striding to the sliding glass rear door of the house, she knocked loudly. No one responded. Through the glass she saw that the family room was equipped with a padded bar, a workout machine and an array of audiovisual equipment. Leaning in one corner was a gleaming surfboard.

The overstuffed couch and chairs were made of leather. On the wall hung posters of female rock stars noted for performing in their underwear.

The whole place screamed Swinging-Bachelor Pad. Jill groaned. Just what she needed—a neighbor who gave loud parties and fancied himself a playboy.

Maybe the new occupants were a family with teenagers, she told herself. At least there'd be parents to keep a lid on the noise.

On her way past the garage, she couldn't resist peering through the window in the side door. The murky light showed one empty space and, in the other, an all-terrain vehicle, the kind overgrown boys took for joyrides in the desert. Skis and ski poles were suspended overhead on hooks.

After a tour around the front to make sure Spike wasn't there, Jill returned home for her car and tried to think like a five-year-old. More specifically, like one very intelligent, independent five-year-old.

She knew he missed his parents. Even a bright child his age didn't necessarily understand that his mom and dad dying meant they could never come back. He might be seeking his old home, except that it was in San Francisco, five hundred miles away.

Down the street she asked some older children on skateboards if they'd seen Spike, giving them a description. They hadn't seen him.

There was a mother with two toddlers at the playground owned by their homeowners' association. She hadn't seen Spike, either.

Twilight was deepening. Now that Daylight Savings Time had ended, darkness came much too soon. What if Spike were lost all night?

Think, Jill, think. He can't have gone far.

Fighting down panic, she reviewed other sites that could be reached by foot from Terrace Crest Estates. There wasn't much that would attract a child—some open land that had once been part of a wholesale nursery and, on the other side, older homes laid out in a flat grid pattern.

Beyond the homes sprawled a low-rise complex of medical buildings. Jill planned to start taking Spike there, but six weeks ago, when he'd had his birthday checkup, he'd still been staying with her mother twenty miles away. So, although she'd pointed it out to him, he wouldn't be familiar with the clinic.

Then she remembered the little shopping center a couple of blocks away. It offered a convenience store, a travel agency, a real estate office and an ice cream parlor. She and Spike had visited it once after he moved in.

He'd been nagging for another treat. Jill wondered if she'd been too strict. In her family there were good reasons to be careful about diet, but she hadn't meant to drive her nephew to desperation.

A few minutes later she pulled into the minimall parking lot. Relief washed through Jill. Spike's head of shiny black hair glowed in the sunshine as he emerged from the ice cream parlor, blissfully licking a cone.

A man followed him out. Tall and lean, the newcomer had sun-warmed brown hair and a few crinkles around his eyes as he smiled down at the boy. The way the maroon sweater stretched across his muscular chest made it evident that, although this man was an inch or so shy of six feet tall, he packed plenty of power.

Why was a stranger buying her nephew ice cream? Jill's throat went dry as the man caught Spike's free hand and led him along the sidewalk.

She was reaching for her cell phone when she remembered her concern about involving the police. Besides, there was no indication that the man had done anything wrong. Gathering her courage, she stepped from the car and marched toward the duo.

The closer she got, the less angry Jill became. Spike's cocky manner of walking made it clear he felt in charge of the situation. Besides, his companion's lopsided smile as he listened to the boy went right to her heart.

"Hi," Jill called. The pair stopped, and Spike gave her a grin full of mischief.

"See what I got!" he said. "It's for my tonsils."

"Your tonsils?" Jill asked.

"They fell out," the man said solemnly. At close range she saw that he had intelligent, gray-green eyes.

Unexpectedly, his assessing gaze made her aware of

herself as a woman...aware of her hair, layered in front and falling softly to her shoulders, and aware of the silk blouse that clung to her breasts. Most of all, aware of the fact that it had been far too long since a man had looked at her this way.

"His tonsils fell out?" she repeated. "That's a creative story, Spike. I doubt this nice man believes it, but it was kind of him to buy you ice cream."

"This isn't ice cream," he said. "It's frozen yogurt. Like you always want me to eat, Aunt Jill."

The man's expression darkened. She was trying to figure out what she'd done wrong, when he said, "You're this boy's guardian?"

"Yes," she said.

"Do you realize this child is too young to wander around unsupervised?" he demanded.

"Of course I realize it. That's why I was—"

He brushed aside her explanation. "You're lucky I didn't call the child protective services."

How dare he lecture her without bothering to find out the facts? She didn't have to justify herself to this stranger.

"I appreciate your looking after him," Jill said crisply. "I'm well aware of my responsibilities, thank you. And I'd be happy to reimburse you for the frozen yogurt, Mr.—?"

"Doctor," he said. "Dr. Markham."

In spite of her annoyance, Jill was impressed by the man's title. That fact made her even more determined to stand up to him. She'd spent four years of marriage being too in awe of her dynamo husband to challenge him about anything.

Never again.

"So how much do I owe you?" To her chagrin, she

realized she'd left her purse in the car. She didn't need to admit that, though, until he named an amount.

"Nothing," he said. "I only hope you've learned a lesson from this experience."

Her cheeks flamed. "I certainly have. Next time, I'll tell the baby-sitter to chain my nephew to a chair so he can't wander off while she's in the other room. That should take care of the problem."

"I didn't realize—" He stopped in confusion.

"You didn't ask, either." Getting a grip on Spike's free arm, Jill led him toward the car. She didn't bother to look back. She doubted the great, arrogant Dr. Markham would stand around making apologies, anyway.

Learn a lesson? She had, indeed. She'd learned which doctor *not* to ask for when she took Spike in for a checkup.

Chapter Two

Chapter Two

Chad stood on the sidewalk with his hands thrust into his pockets, watching Jill's car disappear down the street. He couldn't remember when he'd blown a situation quite this badly.

Not that he'd done any actual harm. Unless you counted ticking off a woman whom he had a strong urge to get to know better.

An impression lingered in his mind of a heart-shaped face, vulnerable blue eyes and unusual silver-blond hair. Every cell in his being had been aware of her full lips, the slender nip in her waist and the elegant curve of her neck.

Getting involved with her would mean too many complications, he told himself with a shake of the head. He admired the woman for taking charge of her nephew, no doubt due to some tragedy or irresponsibility in the family, but Chad had done more than his share of getting involved in other people's problems.

He did wish he hadn't left her with such a bad impression, though. Really, he wasn't just an ego in a white coat.

Feeling chastened, Chad strode through the gathering dusk. His red sports car, a recent acquisition to suit his new lifestyle, awaited him in the clinic parking lot.

"Chad, hold on!" Along the walkway from the internal medicine building came Victor Garcia, M.D. A medical-school friend, he was the one who'd encouraged Chad to join the Flora Vista Medical Clinic last year.

The dark-haired internist whisked over to his late-model SUV and extracted a case of beer from the back seat. "For Sunday's housewarming party. Can't risk letting you run low on essential supplies," he announced as he carted it over.

"My neighbors are going to think I'm a bad influence," Chad grumbled good-naturedly as he opened his postage-stamp-size trunk.

"Hey, why not carry the beer on your ski rack so they can't miss it?" joked his friend. "Better yet, invite them to join us. Any good-looking babes in your development?"

"So far, all I've seen are young mothers and retirees," Chad admitted.

"You ought to move into a condo, like me," Victor said. "The whirlpool's full of pretty ladies every night after work. I should have left my parents' place years ago."

"If I bought a condo, where would I put your dogs?" Chad returned.

Since Vic had decided to move out of his parents' large home at about the same time that Chad's new house went into escrow, he'd talked his friend into taking his two pets, Torero and Blitz. Only after he got them home did Chad discover the dogs were rambunctious and poorly trained.

Yesterday, they'd nearly torn his house apart. Trying

to wear them out, he'd played catch until the ball flew over the fence into his neighbor's yard. Chad supposed he should have asked permission before unlocking the gate, but he'd figured it was best to recover the ball quietly.

"Here's an early housewarming gift." Vic handed him a small box. "It'll help people find your house for the party."

"This isn't hopelessly tacky, is it?" Chad lifted the box gingerly. His friend, although the soul of propriety at work, was known in his off hours for telling risqué jokes and giving gag gifts.

Victor cupped his hands over his heart. "I'm wounded. Tacky? Moi?"

From the box, Chad removed a long silken tube of fabric, obviously a wind sock meant to be flown from his front porch. When he stretched it out, he saw that it showed a dachshund. Or, if a person glanced quickly, it might be mistaken for a certain portion of the male anatomy. "Extremely tacky," he concluded.

"Just put it up on Sunday," Victor said. "Humor me."

"Thanks for the thought. Maybe the dogs can play with it." Chad tossed the wind sock into the back seat. He had no desire to annoy his new neighbors, although he had to admit some of the homeowners' association rules seemed intrusive.

Residents weren't allowed to put up a TV antenna or a satellite dish or to hang a basketball hoop in front of the garage. When they repainted their home's exterior, they had to pick an earth-tone color from a chart approved by the board.

No chain-link fences were allowed, you couldn't grow vegetables in the front yard, nor could you tune up your car in the driveway. Occupants were only permitted to fly a banner or flag three days a year: on the Fourth of July, Flag Day and Memorial Day.

Although Chad wasn't much of a rebel, he chafed at all the restrictions. He supposed he'd get used to them, though.

"I'll see you Sunday afternoon," he said.

"Aren't you coming out on my boat tomorrow?" Vic said. "Noon at the marina, remember? Bring a date if you want."

Chad needed to finish unpacking. On the other hand, the whole point of moving to Flora Vista had been to learn to relax. "Where are we sailing to, anyway?"

"Nowhere in particular. I've got some other friends coming and we'll cruise around the harbor. Nothing strenuous. The object is to do as little as possible as pleasantly as possible."

Chad tried to remember if there had ever been a time in his life, even during his teens, when he'd had such a carefree attitude. He was certain there hadn't.

"I wouldn't miss it," he said.

ACROSS THE KITCHEN TABLE from Jill, Nita Rutledge sipped her tea thoughtfully. Watching her mother, Jill hoped the mention of yesterday's encounter with the doctor, which she'd included casually in her tale of Spike's big adventure, had slipped by unremarked.

"I don't think sneaking out Yvette's front door is a sign of anything serious," she concluded. "Spike's adjusting pretty well, all things considered."

"So what does he look like?" Absentmindedly, her mother patted a short silver curl into place.

"You just saw him a minute ago," Jill said, puzzled. "He smiles a lot. That's a good sign, right?"

"Not Spike. The doctor." Over the edge of the teacup, a pair of bright blue eyes met hers.

Oops. The last thing she wanted was for her mother to start matchmaking. Although she lived a forty-minute drive away, for some purposes it might as well have been next door.

"He's kind of tall," Jill said vaguely. "Not real tall. Brown hair. I thought he had a kind face until he gave me the two-bit lecture."

"A kind face, eh?" Her mother poured more hot water into her cup and dunked a fresh bag of mint tea. "What color eyes?"

"Grayish or greenish or something," Jill said. "I really didn't notice."

"Was he wearing a wedding ring?" she asked.

"Mom!"

"Well, was he?" Nita removed the teabag and set it on her saucer.

"No," Jill conceded.

"Obviously, you noticed *that*," she said with a glint of triumph. "And you say Spike found him at the clinic? So he works close by."

"You forgot to mention that doctors earn a good income," Jill said, keeping her tone light. "That should make him a great catch."

"Having enough money for your needs is important," said her mother. "Having a lot of money isn't always such a good thing, though. With some men, as we both know, it goes to their heads."

Gary Voss, Jill's former husband, had made a small fortune in business. In the process he'd become self-centered and insensitive to the point of betraying his wife when she needed him most.

The question that troubled Jill was whether there'd

been signs, right from the beginning, of her husband's poor character. Had she been so impressed by his achievements and his good looks that she'd been blinded to the obvious? Or, worse, could such a flawed nature remain undetectable until too late?

In three years she hadn't been able to bring herself to trust another man. She wasn't sure what it would take to break down the wall she'd built, and she wasn't eager to find out. She certainly didn't intend to start with the Dr. Jekyll and Mr. Hyde she'd met yesterday.

"There's no point in speculating, Mom," she said. "I'm never going to see Dr. Markham again. Plus he's probably got a girlfriend, or two or three."

"Two or three is better than one," said her mother. "If he has only one, that could be serious. But I'm not pushing. If something was meant to happen between the two of you, it will."

Jill knew perfectly well that this wasn't the end of her mother's interest in the good doctor. True, Nita probably wouldn't broach the subject again for a while. But she would think about it, and her daughter could almost always tell what she was thinking.

"So, how are you eating these days?" A nutritionist, Nita Rutledge took a keen interest in her daughter's health. "High fiber, low fat, low sugar?"

"Of course," Jill said. "Have you seen the new bran muffin baking mixes? Even Spike likes them."

Mercifully the subject matter stayed away from Dr. Markham for the next half hour, until Nita left to pick up a food donation from a nearby supermarket. On Saturdays she volunteered in a program that distributed food packages to the working poor.

As her mother gave Spike a farewell hug, Jill saw tears glistening in Nita's eyes. Losing a son and daughter-in-law in a car crash had been hard on her. She'd tried to give her grandson a home, but had been forced to admit after a few months that she was no longer attuned to being a full-time mom.

Jill wasn't so sure about her own capabilities in that department. But she loved this little guy, and she was going to make a home for him, no matter how many bumps they encountered along the way.

After his grandma left, Spike petted Normal, scratching behind his ears the way Jill had shown him. In the past month, the boy had grown attached to the cats.

"Where's Neurotic?" he asked.

"I haven't seen her this morning." The black-and-white adventurer had eaten her food last night, but then she must have gone out. "Shall we check the backyard?"

"I'll put my shoes on!"

When they stepped outside, Jill got angry all over again at the new neighbor and his unruly dogs. Last night it had been too dark for her to do any gardening, and the mess looked even worse this morning as the flowers shriveled.

"Did Neurotic do this?" Spike asked. "Boy, is she in trouble!"

"No, a couple of dogs did this," Jill grumbled. "And their owner owes me an apology, to say the least."

The dogs had been barking and growling for the last half hour, out of sight behind the fence. She wondered what would be the best way to deal with her inconsiderate new neighbor. The last thing she wanted was to start World War III over the back fence, but she shouldn't have to put up with this racket.

"It's Neurotic!" cried her nephew. "Look!"

Jill followed his gaze uphill to the other yard. Atop the gazebo roof that covered the whirlpool bath perched the black-and-white cat. From below her came the howls of the two dogs.

"Their owner must be playing his stereo so loud he can't hear them," she grumbled.

"We have to help her down," Spike said.

It didn't appear to Jill that her cat was in any immediate danger. And, she had to admit, it wasn't the neighbor's fault if her cat had strayed into his yard.

Then she saw that the gate was ajar. Neurotic might have been chased right out of her yard.

Pure hot anger spurted through Jill. How dare someone open the gate a second time? He must be the most inconsiderate person in Flora Vista.

In the yard above hers, she heard a glass door slide open and a masculine voice call, "Hey, boys! What are you up to?" A chorus of barks responded, along with a plaintive meow. "Oh, having a little fun, eh?" the man said. "Well, that ought to keep you amused for a while."

Amused? His dogs were terrifying her cat! Well, perhaps terrify was too strong a word, since Neurotic's daring was legendary. She'd been known to challenge small canines to a fight, if only to prove she was still the fastest slasher in the West. But this was two against one.

As she stalked toward the open gate, Jill tried to ignore the funny feeling in her stomach. Something about the man's voice had rung a bell.

It didn't matter. She was completely in the right. To heck with finding a diplomatic approach.

TWO THINGS OCCURRED TO CHAD as a stunning silver-blonde in tight jeans and a figure-hugging pink turtle-neck sweater stomped into his yard. The first was that he was glad to see Spike's aunt again. The second was that he'd forgotten to lock the gate.

Beside her jogged her small, plucky nephew. A big smile spread across his face. "Hi, Chad!"

Jill halted abruptly. "Oh, no."

He wished she didn't sound so dismayed. "Hi, Spike and Aunt Jill. I guess we must be neighbors."

"That's my cat." Shading her eyes, she frowned to-ward the gazebo. "The one your dogs are trying to tear apart."

"They're having a little harmless fun," he said.

"I suppose you think it serves me right for letting my cat run around *unsupervised*," she retorted, using his own word from yesterday. "Except for the inciden-tal fact that you opened the gate and let your dogs tear up my yard and chase Neurotic out of her own home."

"Neurotic?" he said. "Don't people give cats sim-ple names like Patches and Felix anymore?"

He knew it was unfair to ignore her complaint. Still, Chad enjoyed the way her eyes flashed and her chest heaved. A fiery woman like her would be all the sweeter when she melted in his arms....

This was crazy. The woman lived directly behind him, for heaven's sake. Getting involved with her would be like laying a picnic blanket atop a wasp's nest.

On the other hand, he liked a challenge. He hoped she did, too.

"This situation strikes you as humorous?" Jill snapped. "After your lecture about responsibility, I'd think it would have occurred to you that leaving the gate open exposes my nephew to your unfenced whirl-pool."

Chad allowed himself a few seconds to feel like a complete idiot. It wasn't an entirely unfamiliar sensation, but rare enough to be of interest.

"You're right," he said. "I apologize. From now on, I'll make a point of keeping the gate locked. I've also ordered a safety cover for the whirlpool, the kind that sounds an alarm if anyone disturbs it." To Spike he added, "Never, never go into a pool without a grown-up."

"Why not? Does it have a crocodile in it?" the little boy asked hopefully.

Chad knelt close to him and looked into his eyes. "Spike, some things don't look dangerous, but they are. Water looks like fun, doesn't it?"

The boy nodded.

"And you don't see how it could hurt you, do you?"

"No," he said.

"Well, it can." Chad searched for a way to explain so a child could understand. "Sometimes water is deeper than it looks. And the jets of the whirlpool could turn on and the suction—that's a force that pulls you down—can hold you under. It would be awful not to be able to breathe, wouldn't it?"

"Or the dogs might jump in and knock me down," Spike said, getting into the spirit of "what-iffing." "Or I could slip and hit my head."

"Lots of things could go wrong," Chad agreed. "That's why you should never go into the water without a grown-up."

"Okay," the boy said solemnly. "Now can I see your house?"

"First I'd better take care of the dogs before they

commit caticide.'' After rising, he grabbed the pair by their collars. ''Torero! Blitz! Let's put you two in the garage.''

''Torero and Blitz?'' Jill said. ''And you're complaining about a cat named Neurotic?''

He decided not to mention who had actually chosen the names. Vic wasn't here to defend himself.

Dragging the less-than-cooperative animals, Chad shut them in the garage. By the time he got back to the yard, the black-and-white cat had disappeared, and Jill was guiding Spike toward the gate. ''We can see his house another time,'' she told the boy.

Disappointment echoed inside Chad. He didn't want her to leave yet, and he didn't like the fact that he'd once again made himself look bad. ''I'm sorry about the gate. How much damage did the dogs do?''

''You can see for yourself if you care to look,'' she told him. ''I'll have to buy at least a flat of flowers, and it'll take weeks for the lawn to recover.''

''I'll be happy to pay—''

''Just don't let it happen again.'' She ducked through the gap and replaced the lock.

The least she could do was give him a chance to make amends, Chad thought. After all, they were neighbors.

He strolled over and leaned against the gate, watching her and the boy descend the sloping rear portion of their yard. The marks of Torero's and Blitz's rampage were unmistakable.

''I can fix this,'' Chad called. He didn't know much about gardening, but he could figure it out, and it would be fun with Spike helping.

Then he remembered that he'd promised to go boating in a little over an hour. Great. If she took him up on his offer and he reneged, she would figure he was insincere, along with all his other faults.

JILL WAS TEMPTED to let Chad do the dirty work. The sight of the doctor kneeling in her yard with smudges on his arrogant face would almost be worth the aggravation of having to converse with him further.

Almost but not quite. "No, thanks!" she called, then crouched to wedge a clump of daisies into place in the flower bed. Since the roots were intact, the flowers might survive. "I guess we've got our work cut out for us in the garden today, right, Spike?"

"I can help!" he said.

"You sure can," Jill said. "Let's decide how many new flowers we need, and you can pick out the colors at the nursery."

"I have an excellent color sense," called their neighbor, still hanging over the gate. "I'd be happy to choose for you, and buy the flowers, too, although it'll have to wait a few days until I have time."

"Choose for me?" Jill straightened and planted her hands on her hips. "Why is it that when men pay the bills, they assume they get to make all the decisions? Even when they're paying off a debt?"

"I'm offering you my decorating expertise, free of charge," Chad said cheerfully. "That isn't 'making all the decisions,' it's providing a service."

Jill wished he didn't look so delightfully audacious, his grayish or greenish or whatever-they-were eyes dancing as he awaited her reaction. "I've seen your decorating expertise, through your patio door," she returned. "If I decide to open a bordello, I'll be sure to call you."

"What's a bordello?" asked Spike.

"Yes, what's a bordello?" Chad parroted with mock innocence.

Next door, the creak of Yvette's side gate and the sound of raised voices saved Jill the necessity of making a ticklish explanation. It didn't take more than a few words before she recognized the strident tones of neighbor and homeowner's board member Louise Norwalk, or perhaps it was her twin, Lorraine.

"You've either got to finish that—what do you call it?—shade house or tear it down," the woman said.

"I do plan to finish it," Yvette protested softly. "But my arthritis has been hurting, now that the weather's turned cooler. Besides, it's in my backyard, so I don't see why it concerns the homeowners' association."

"The way it's positioned on your slope, it's visible from the street," said the other sister.

"Only if you stand to one side, crane your neck and snoop!" Jill announced, loudly enough for them to hear.

For as long as Jill had lived here, the two women had been badgering Yvette, who privately referred to them as the Flora Dora Girls. The twins, charter residents of the development, took their positions on the board much too seriously.

They claimed that, as real estate agents, they were concerned about damage to property values. She believed they simply enjoyed imposing their taste on others.

Peering over the wall, she saw Louise—the one with short hair—and Lorraine, who wore her chestnut hair at chin length, towering over Yvette. The twins, who appeared to be in their forties, wrinkled their noses as they regarded the rear yard.

"Jill, tell me how can you stand this mess next door?" demanded Louise. "You must see it every time you look over the...my goodness, what happened to your yard?"

"My dogs happened to her yard," said Chad, who had a good view from his position on higher ground. "Our attorneys are negotiating a settlement at this very moment."

Lorraine brightened. "Oh, you're the *doctor!* Welcome to the Terrace Crest Estates! It's the best development in the city of Flora Vista, and we intend to keep it that way."

"Exactly what's wrong with this shade house?" He turned his attention to the half-finished latticework structure. Up one side wove a pink-flowered vine that was blooming deliriously. "It looks picturesque to me."

"When it's finished, it will be a lovely place to take tea in the afternoon," Yvette added.

"It's a shambles!" said Lorraine. "Look at it, doctor. Why, it's practically a health hazard. I was driving by with a client the other day, and she said, 'Good heavens, what's that?'"

"Did she require hospitalization?" Chad inquired. "I mean, seeing as it's such a health menace."

Against her wishes, Jill found herself liking this man. He wasn't so bad when he turned his sense of humor on someone else.

"You're new here, Doctor," Louise reproved. "Once you get a better feel for the place, you'll understand."

"Maybe so." Jill hoped Chad would say more, but, apparently losing interest, he ambled toward his own house.

So much for counting on his support. She supposed the man liked to take cheap shots, then duck out before there were repercussions.

"Since I live next door, I'm the one primarily affected," she told the twins. "And I don't object."

"You won't be so indifferent when this eyesore attracts pests." Lorraine made a sweeping gesture, as if assorted beasts were likely to jump from the bushes at any moment. "There are wild animals around here who make their homes in things like that. Raccoons, skunks, possums, not to mention rats and mice."

"There are no rats and mice here. My cat patrols both our yards," Jill said. "As for the other animals, I fail to see why they'd be more attracted to an unfinished shade house than to a completed one."

"Yvette should have sought board permission before building anything on the slope," Louise retorted. "If it's visible from the street, even barely, it comes under our jurisdiction. Whoa! That can't be what I think it is!"

She was staring uphill toward Chad's house. As Jill turned, she heard a soft flapping sound in the breeze, and then she saw it.

Standing on a ladder, Chad was attaching a wind sock to his gazebo roof. At first, Jill couldn't believe it showed what she thought it did, but the tan shape was unmistakably a portion of the male anatomy.

"That's—that's indecent!" cried Louise.

"Haven't seen one of those in years," said Yvette, although whether she was referring to the wind sock or to its subject matter remained unclear.

"It's a little doggy," said Spike, who was sitting on a planter playing with Neurotic.

Jill squinted and realized he was right. The sausage

shape painted onto the wind sock had four short legs and two floppy ears.

From his imperial perch on the ladder, Chad called, "Maybe it would look better on the roof. What do you think, ladies? That way people could see it from the front yard."

The Flora Dora Girls muttered to each other. "It *is* a dog," Lorraine said.

"It's scurrilous!"

"I agree, it makes a bad impression, but—"

"Shocking! People will have accidents, staring at it."

"It might even give them ideas," Yvette said. "Good ideas."

To Jill's relief, Chad reeled in the wind sock and climbed down. "I don't think that shade house looks so bad by comparison, do you, folks?"

"We're coming over to talk to you," said Lorraine. "I think we need to get clear on a few matters, Dr. Markham."

On the ground he gave a fatalistic shrug. "I'd love to, but I'm going sailing."

"On a boat?" Spike asked wistfully. "I've never been on a boat."

"In fact," Chad said, "Jill and Spike and I are going sailing. In about five minutes."

"I never—" Jill stopped. She didn't want to argue in front of these suddenly very interested observers. If there was anything the Flora Dora Girls loved more than taking charge of other people's property, it was gossip.

"Don't forget to put on rubber-soled shoes," Chad said. "And bring a sweater for Spike. It gets cold on the water." He disappeared into his house.

The boy jumped up and down with excitement. Jill didn't want to disappoint him. She'd intended to find interesting things for the two of them to do on weekends, hadn't she? And she could hardly take the boy sailing by herself.

She supposed she could put up with Chad's company for a few more hours. She just hoped he didn't plan to fly the wind sock from the mast.

Chapter Three

Bringing Jill and Spike Rutledge to one of Victor Garcia's bachelor outings might not have been the best idea he'd ever had, Chad reflected as they strolled along the boardwalk that edged the marina. His friend *had* said to bring a date, though.

The wistful look on the little boy's face had been impossible to resist. And the way Jill kept pushing Chad away brought out his fighting spirit.

He sampled the scents of brine and seaweed. To his left the water of the harbor rippled lazily in the sunshine, while overhead a seagull wheeled with a catlike cry.

On the water a sloop glided by, its many-hued sail filling with the light breeze. At their moorings, yachts bobbed between catamarans, powerboats and old-fashioned sailing vessels. Dock space at the marina, in a seaside town about twenty-five miles from Flora Vista, was at a premium.

"So are those women I met the heads of the home-owners' association?" Chad asked as they passed a bikini and surf shop.

"A fellow named Sam Wright is the chairman, but they're both on the board," Jill said. "I'm afraid you've made a pair of ruthless enemies. They'll find some way to harass you.''

"I'll make sure to give them a range of infringements to choose from," Chad replied, looking forward to the battle.

"Are we going anywhere in particular today?" she asked.

He shook his head. "Just around the harbor."

"Whose sailboat is it?" A puff of air lifted Jill's hair, making it glint of silver and gold in the sunlight.

"It's not actually a sailboat. That would be too much work. It's a powerboat," Chad corrected. "It belongs to Vic Garcia, a friend from medical school at UCLA. He's the one who lured me to Flora Vista last year."

"So we have him to blame," she said dryly.

"Do people live on these boats?" Spike's eyes were wide with fascination.

"A few people do. They have to get a special permit, I think." Although he wasn't much of a sailor, Chad had grown up in the Los Angeles area and been invited onto friends' boats often enough to glean a little knowledge of them.

"I'd like to live on a boat," the boy said. "Then you could take your house with you, wherever you go."

The comment reminded Chad that Spike must have left his own home behind when he moved in with his aunt. "Where are you from, little guy?"

"San Francisco," he said. "They've got boats there, too. My daddy promised we'd get one when I'm older."

Jill bit her lip and glanced away. Chad could see that whatever had happened to Spike's family had been painful for her.

"Here we are." At the pier Chad opened a gate and held it for his companions.

"Look at me! I can walk on water!" cried Spike, skipping along the pier. The boards creaked beneath his movements and, below, water slapped the pilings.

When Jill moved past Chad, an old-fashioned fragrance transported him to a field of violets. Among them moved a silver-blond nymph, her laughing eyes daring him to take her.

His body tightened, and he had to force himself to close the gate and walk calmly after her. His big hands would fit neatly around her small waist, he noted. Before she knew it, he could spin her around and steal a kiss.

He wouldn't, of course. Not in full view of Spike and half a dozen weekend sailors. Still, Chad tucked the impulse away for later, when he might find himself in a position to do something about it.

THE SCENTS AND SOUNDS of the harbor hit Jill harder than she'd expected. Gary's high-tech consulting firm had owned a boat that they'd used fairly often.

They'd sailed out of a different harbor, farther south. But the smell of ocean water and the scrape of boats at their moorings carried her back to the days when she'd trusted a ruggedly handsome man with dark-blond hair and blue eyes.

Jill straightened her shoulders. She'd grown far beyond that naive younger self. There was no point in spoiling her outing with regrets.

"Here it is." Chad touched her elbow. They'd come alongside a powerboat named *Lady of Leisure*.

On the rear deck a man and a woman in shorts and T-shirts lounged along padded, built-in benches. The man's hair was buzz cut like a marine's, while the woman's blond-streaked brown hair whipped in the breeze.

"Hi, I'm Chad," the doctor said. "Is Vic around?"

"Belowdecks, matie," said the man. "I'm Aaron and this is Shelly."

Chad introduced Jill and Spike and swung onto the boat. He lifted the boy easily onboard, then extended his hand to Jill.

His strong grip closed over her hand and, as she jumped up beside him, he caught her waist to steady her. A silvery tremor ran along her skin.

She could feel the masculine power coiled inside him. The contact made her light-headed, and she clung to him for a moment before letting go.

Chad released her slowly. "I'd better go find Vic."

"Could you ask if he's got a child-size life jacket?" Jill said.

Aaron crooked an eyebrow. "Even in the harbor?" he asked. "That's carrying things to extremes, wouldn't you say?"

Jill instantly disliked him, although she knew it was irrational. After all, she'd met other people who considered her to be overly cautious about safety.

Chad came to her defense. "I think we should all wear life jackets. The harbor isn't a wading pool." Jill could have hugged him.

"Would you care for a beer?" Shelly asked as Chad disappeared into the boat's interior. "We've got some soft drinks for your son."

Jill didn't bother correcting the false impression. Besides, Spike *was* her son now. "Thanks. And do you have any diet soda for me?"

"Help yourself." Shelly gestured toward a cooler.

"Diet soda?" Aaron muttered. "What's wrong with beer?"

Ignoring him, Jill found a caffeine-free soda for Spike and a sugar-free one for herself and was opening the cans when Chad popped out of the cabin. He was followed by a dark-haired man with an infectious smile.

This, she learned, was Vic, and he seemed delighted rather than annoyed to have a child along for the trip. As soon as introductions were made, he promised to let Spike help him steer the boat.

His girlfriend, a pretty brunette named Cara, turned out to be equally pleasant. Maybe this outing wasn't such a bad idea, Jill decided as she helped her nephew into his life jacket and put one on herself. Chad, Vic and Cara also put on jackets, but Aaron and Shelly waved them away.

They all chose sandwiches from another cooler, and after they ate, Vic cast off from the dock. He, Cara and an elated Spike climbed a short ladder to the top of the boat, where the controls were located.

Sitting below with Chad, Jill felt the thrum of the engine as they swung out of the marina into the broad harbor. The boat maneuvered around other craft, keeping within the posted speed of five knots, which Jill recalled were nautical miles per hour.

Sails dotted the harbor as other weekend sailors enjoyed the mild November weather. The hot Santa Ana winds that blew in from the desert had ended last month, and the winter rains hadn't yet begun.

As they glided forward, the occupants of *Lady of Leisure* had a splendid view of the palatial homes edging the harbor. One white, castle-like structure glimmered as if studded with diamonds. Several sprawling modern homes seemed almost entirely made of glass, while their residents sunbathed on harborfront decks.

In his chair Chad stretched his long legs and leaned back, closing his eyes against the sunshine. His navy slacks, orange vest and off-white crewneck sweater outlined a body that might have been sculpted for a Greek temple.

Jill relished the memory of him taunting the Flora Dora Girls. The man had taken Yvette's side against her tormenters, without knowing the details. It spoke well for him, even if he had shot off his mouth at her yesterday.

As they wove through the harbor, the tension of the work week seeped away. The only fly in her ointment was Aaron, who, between swigs of beer, made derogatory comments to Shelly about other boaters and about colleagues at the pharmaceuticals firm where the two of them worked.

At last Chad sat up and stretched. His face, averted from Aaron, showed annoyance at this constant stream of complaints.

"Care for a tour of the cabins, and then we could go up top with Spike?" he asked.

"You bet!"

To reach the interior, they dropped down a long step. Jill half expected Chad to brace her, and experienced a twinge of disappointment when he didn't.

The boat had a compact aft cabin with a bench that opened into a bed. The large center cabin contained a complete galley, a collapsible dinette table and another foldout bed. Beyond it lay the bathroom, which Jill remembered was called the head, and a small forward cabin used for storage.

"Does your friend own his boat?" she asked, impressed.

"With a little help from the bank," Chad said. "He saved his money by staying at his parents' home until recently, when he moved into a condo. I decided I'd rather own a house and skip the boat."

Jill wondered why he wanted a whole house to himself, but decided not to ask. Most likely he considered it a good investment. She doubted he'd bought one for the reason she'd bought hers: to make a nest that she could retreat to.

They exited into the bright sunshine and climbed the ladder to the roof. At the control console, Vic sat with Spike on his lap, letting the boy help steer.

"Look, Aunt Jill!" he cried. "I'm the captain!"

"You sure are." Up here, Jill could feel the wind tangling her hair, but she didn't care. It was worth it to see her nephew having a good time.

"He's a sweetie," Cara said from her bench seat. "Does he live with you?"

"I'm adopting him." Jill hesitated to say more in the boy's hearing.

"Watch out!" Vic pointed to their left. "That's a Harbor Patrol boat. It's like a police cruiser. We don't want them giving us a ticket."

"You mean there are rules?" Spike asked. "Even on the water?"

"It's tough, isn't it?" Vic said. "A man can hardly find a place to cut loose anymore. Although we try, don't we, Chad?"

"We do our best," he agreed.

Jill remembered the surfboard in Chad's den and the skis and ATV in his garage. Most likely the reason he wanted his own house was so he'd have room to store all his toys, she reflected.

These guys must spend all their spare time living out a bachelor's dream life. She couldn't fault them for it, since neither had family obligations.

If she ever met the right man, though, he would have to be someone she could rely on. Just because Chad had a high-flying lifestyle like her ex-husband's didn't mean he was equally untrustworthy, but the information put Jill on her guard.

"You don't have to entertain my nephew all day," she told Vic.

"I'm enjoying it," he said. "Maybe I should have been a pediatrician instead of an internist. After growing up the eldest in a family of six, I miss playing with kids."

"There's a solution to that problem," Cara hinted broadly. "If you ever decide to settle down."

Vic circled his neck with his hands, noose-like, and pretended to gag.

"Subtle, isn't he?" said Chad.

"The two of us nearly killed ourselves getting through medical school, internship and residency," Vic said. "We deserve some fun, right, partner?"

"I'm a couple of years behind you in the fun department," Chad said. "I've got a lot to make up for."

"Did I mention we're going to Las Vegas next weekend?" Vic asked. "Four or five of us. You, too. No excuses."

"I think I've got next Saturday off," Chad agreed. "Sure, that sounds great."

Jill had to work that day, not that anyone had asked her to go to Vegas. Nor would she have wanted to, she told herself, bracing her legs and swaying with the boat as it navigated a bend in the channel.

"You've been sailing before, I take it," Chad said. "You seem to have your sea legs."

"My ex-husband's company had a boat." She didn't elaborate. She certainly didn't want to run down her ex-husband. Without knowing anything about the man, Chad might assume she was simply bitter.

"You two ought to catch some rays on the foredeck," Vic said. "You'll get a great view up there."

Jill was grateful for the suggestion, since she had no desire to share any more of Aaron's company on the rear deck. "Sure," she said. "Sounds like a plan."

The two of them retreated down the ladder and walked along a narrow side deck to the front. Jill inhaled deeply the salty air and watched with interest as they approached the mouth of the harbor.

Once past the breakwater, a boat could voyage to Santa Catalina Island a few hours offshore, or hug the coast north to Santa Barbara or south to Laguna Beach. The water got rougher out there, though, and Jill was glad they were staying in the harbor.

They climbed onto the foredeck, which reminded her of the extended hood of a car. Cold spray flecked Jill's face, taking the edge off the midday heat.

She sat on the deck with her back to a porthole. From here she couldn't see Spike's position on top of the boat without standing up and twisting around, but she trusted Vic to look after him.

"Your friend is great with kids," she said.

"He's a little wild but he has a good heart." Chad sat a few feet away, resting against another porthole. He had, in profile, a straight nose and a classic chin, Jill noticed, and quickly looked away.

As they sped forward, the nearness of the water and the sensation of cutting through the waves gave her a small rush. She used to be much bolder when she was younger, Jill reflected. She'd gone up with Gary in his small plane several times and had considered taking flying lessons herself.

The discovery of her own vulnerability had come suddenly and painfully. Until now, she hadn't realized quite how cautious it had made her.

"This feels good," she said.

"That's the point," Chad replied.

"It sounds as if you two lead a swinging lifestyle." She hoped he wouldn't take that as criticism. "I mean, it's okay to have a good time."

He rotated his shoulders, getting the kinks out. Even in a life jacket, Chad was a tempting sight. Imagining how those muscles would feel under her hands, Jill was glad to be sitting a safe distance away.

"You sound as if it's only okay for other people," he said.

"It never occurred to me to let loose after my divorce. If anything, I hunkered down and worked harder."

"You bought the house yourself?" Chad asked.

"I used my settlement as a down payment," she admitted. "I'm the assistant marketing director at the Flora Vista Mall. It pays enough to cover my mortgage and expenses, but I couldn't have saved up for a house."

"How about your nephew? Where does he fit into the picture?" Chad asked.

"It's kind of a long story." *And a painful one,* she added silently.

"I'd like to hear it, if you don't mind," he said.

Why not? As her neighbor, he'd be seeing a lot of Spike, and the story wasn't exactly a secret.

Taking a deep breath, Jill plunged ahead. "My brother, Ellery, was an investment counselor in San Francisco. Six months ago he and his wife were driving to Lake Tahoe for a business meeting when he lost control of the car. It flipped and killed them both."

Jill would never forget the shock of receiving the news by phone from her mother. Even now, tears blurred her vision.

"I'm so sorry, Jill. Was Spike in the car?"

"They'd left him with friends," she said. "Thank goodness." As she spoke the boat curved around a buoy that marked the end of the harbor and headed back.

"And you decided to take him in?" Chad said. "That was a major change for you."

"First he went to live with my mother in Costa Mesa," Jill explained. "Much as she loves him, she has a busy schedule and had a hard time adjusting to his needs. It wasn't a good situation for either of them. I wasn't sure I was ready to take on a child, but life doesn't always suit itself to our plans, does it?"

"When did he come to live with you?"

"About a month ago," she said. "We've been adjusting the best we can. He wandered away from the baby-sitter, as you saw."

"How do you feel about him?" Chad asked. "I mean, it can't be an easy situation."

"I love him." It was the first time Jill had spoken those words aloud. "And in spite of the inconveniences, he's good for me. After my divorce I got too wrapped up in my own hurts. Now someone else needs me, and it forces me to rise above myself."

"What's Spike's real name, anyway?" he asked.

"Leon," she said. "He hates it, even though I tell him it sounds like a lion."

"He'll grow into it."

The vessel rocked as if people were moving around on the upper deck. Chad got up to take a look.

"Apparently Spike got tired of steering," he said. "He and Cara just went inside, and Vic's turning over the helm to Aaron."

"Is that safe, considering how much beer he's had?" Jill asked. "How well do you know Aaron, anyway?"

"First time I've met him. Vic has a lot of friends," Chad said.

"I guess we've sat here long enough." She'd enjoyed having Chad's undivided attention, she admitted silently, and telling him Spike's story hadn't been as painful as she'd expected, but it was time to get moving. "I'd like to check on Spike."

"Want a hand?"

"I'm all right." She was getting up when the engine noise rose and the boat picked up speed. Jostled against the porthole, Jill had to put out a hand to steady herself.

"Hey!" Chad shouted upward. "Slow down!"

Instead, the boat veered to one side, then the other, as if Aaron were showing off. Jill grabbed on to the railing. "What is that maniac doing?"

"You were right about the alcohol," Chad said. "Vic should never have let him drive."

They swerved around a rowboat, nearly swamping it with their wake. Ahead loomed a yacht. If they hit the other boat, Jill realized, she and Chad would fly right into it, with neither restraints nor helmets to protect them.

At the last minute, they spun past the yacht with a

few feet to spare. From the bridge she heard Aaron shout, "Yahoo!"

"Hang on!" Chad told her. "I'm going up there to stop him." She had to lip read half his words, because the wind carried them away.

It was risky for him to climb atop the boat while it was moving so erratically. "Why don't you let Vic handle it?" she asked.

"He should have done something by now. Maybe he got hurt while Aaron was jerking us around." Heavy traffic in a channel leading to the marina forced them to slow, and Chad seized the opportunity to stand up. "Hold tight."

She wanted to protest again as he scrambled onto the top of the boat. But what if Vic had hit his head and needed medical attention? And someone had to take the controls away from Aaron.

Jill was so angry she could hardly hold still. How dare that creep risk other people's safety? And why had Vic entrusted him with the boat in the first place?

Ahead, a gap opened between two sailboats, and the *Lady of Leisure* shot forward. She hoped Chad could keep his balance as he reached the top.

"Yippee!" Aaron yelled again, and the boat began weaving in a tight *S* shape. Shelly was shouting at him, loud enough to be heard over the wind. The few intelligible words scorched Jill's ears, but apparently had no effect on the lout.

At one side of the marina, a Harbor Patrol boat peeled away from the dock. She wondered what the patrolmen could do in a case like this. Board the ship while it was veering around? Ram them?

She heard a scuffing noise overhead as Chad crossed the roof, and then his deep voice ordered Aaron to relinquish the helm. "Who's gonna make me?" came the arrogant response.

The patrol boat was heading their way. Over a loudspeaker, the captain ordered Aaron to stand down. There was no response.

"Let go, now!" Chad said.

"Come on, Aaron. Give him the wheel!" Shelly called.

"He can come and get it," taunted the drunk.

Jill's muscles stiffened as she waited for the sounds of a fight. Someone could get injured up there.

She hoped it wouldn't be Chad.

Chapter Four

Chad vaulted a railing into the cockpit. He was close enough now for Aaron to take a swing at him.

The other man was a few inches taller and a bit heavier, but most of the weight lay around his midsection. Even so, they were evenly matched.

The important thing was to keep the boat from hitting anything or dislodging one of its occupants. Where, Chad wondered for the umpteenth time, was Vic, and if he'd been hurt, how badly?

"Don't you think you've done enough damage?" he said in the level voice that he'd learned to use with belligerent patients during a stint in an emergency room. "You won't gain anything by fighting me."

"Vic gave me the boat," came the sneering response. "It's my toy and I can play with it."

"He's really drunk," Shelly said from behind him.

"Shut up!" the man snarled at her.

Chad's throat tightened. He hoped these two didn't have an abusive relationship. He wasn't sure he could stop himself from punching the man if he lashed out at Shelly.

"Don't you talk to me that way!" the young woman returned, unafraid. "You're making a complete idiot of yourself, Aaron. You see those harbor patrolmen?" She indicated the cruiser that had pulled alongside. "They can haul you off to jail. And I'll make sure everybody at work hears about it, too."

Uncertainty shaded the man's beefy face. "Aw, don't make a federal case out of it. I was just having a little fun."

After a brief hesitation he relinquished the helm to Chad. The patrolmen called for the engine to be shut down, and he complied.

One of the officers came onboard, his manner courteous but unamused. A minute later Cara emerged from belowdecks with a pale-faced Spike.

"Vic hit his head when that…that jerk Aaron decided to play cowboy," she announced. "Chad, could you take a look at him?"

"Shall I call the paramedics?" the patrolman asked.

"I'm a doctor," Chad said. "Let me take a look first."

He found his friend suffering from a headache but with no signs of a concussion. "I'm sorry," Vic said. "I figured Aaron could handle the boat for a few minutes. Spike got sick to his stomach and I wanted to make sure he was all right."

"Is he?"

"Minus his lunch, but otherwise okay," Vic said.

"You may be, too, but let's not count on it. Someone needs to watch you for a few hours," Chad said. They both knew there was some danger of brain swelling after a head injury. "Will Cara be with you?"

Vic nodded, then winced. "I know the drill."

On deck Chad found a chastened Aaron watching the patrolman take out his ticket book. Jill had joined Cara and was hugging Spike and apologizing.

"I should have realized you might get sick," she said.

"I was fine most of the time," the little boy protested.

"He handled himself beautifully," Cara said, then turned on Aaron. "A lot better than some grown-ups I could name. Here this little boy was manfully trying to hold it in, and then you started flinging the boat all over the harbor. Not to mention that Vic whacked his head and nearly got coldcocked."

"What's the use of a boat if you can't have fun with it?" Aaron demanded.

"Excuse me, sir," the patrolman said. "I'm going to have to check your blood-alcohol level."

The bluster faded from Aaron's stance. Chad wasn't sure whether drunken boating was treated as severely as drunken driving, but no doubt the penalties were stiff.

Across the harbor, someone began shouting. A couple of horns sounded, and the patrolman turned.

"Boat sinking. Get on board," called his companion on the cruiser.

The officer shot Aaron a quelling look, finished writing his ticket and handed it to him. "You're getting off easy this time. Don't let there be a next time," he said, and departed.

Shelly made a face. "What's it for, reckless driving and speeding? You were luckier than you deserve."

Aaron wiped his forehead. "I didn't need a drunk driving conviction."

Vic came out of the cabin, pressing an ice bag to his head. "That wasn't cool, what you did," he said. "Risking my boat, not to mention our lives."

"I didn't think it was dangerous." Aaron held up

his hands placatingly. "Hey, man, I'm sorry. I won't do it again."

"You sure won't," Vic muttered. "Chad, can you dock the boat for me?"

"Just point me to the right berth."

Once they were tied down, he found Jill cradling Spike on a padded bench. The little boy sat up when he saw Chad.

"I only got a little bit sick," he said.

"Even some of the best sailors get seasick once in a while," Chad said.

"It felt icky when we were banging around," Spike admitted. "Like one of those big carnival rides."

"I'll bet you could use a dose of my favorite medicine. Ice cream."

The little face brightened. "Yeah!"

Jill gave Chad an appreciative smile. He was glad she wasn't angry at him for railroading her into coming along on this expedition.

He didn't regret bringing her, though. They'd had a chance to talk, and he'd found that he liked her even more than he expected.

She'd taken in her nephew, despite being unprepared, and clearly loved him. At conferences and medical society meetings, Chad had met a lot of people who talked a big story about saving the world and making things better for the children, but all too few were willing to make the personal sacrifices to meet a child's needs themselves, day by day.

After making sure Vic wasn't becoming dizzy or disoriented, Chad thanked him for the trip and accompanied Jill and Spike along the boardwalk to an ice cream shop. "I'm taking you guys out for dinner when we get home," he said, "but right now I think a little something in Spike's stomach would be better than a full meal.''

"As long as it's ice cream.'' The boy gave a skip.

"You don't have to buy us dinner," Jill said.

"I'd like to. Consider it compensation for your wild ride.''

Her blue eyes meet his. "That was brave, the way you faced that man.''

"It had to be done." Chad never sought out confrontations, but he didn't shrink from them, either. "You can't turn your back on a situation like that.''

"Some people will go to almost any length to avoid unpleasantness. Especially their own.'' From Jill's faraway gaze, he guessed she was thinking of her ex-husband.

She'd mentioned being absorbed in her own hurts after the divorce. What had the man done to her?

Whatever it was, she's handling it fine. She doesn't need you prying into her affairs.

He had too soft a heart, Chad knew. Or maybe he'd simply been naive and arrogant when he was younger, to think he could solve other people's problems. He hadn't had much success playing Superman in the past, and he didn't intend to try again anytime soon.

The ice cream restored Spike's spirits, and on the drive home he chattered about the things Vic had told him. Words like "helm," "rudder" and "starboard" flew from his mouth.

"The kid's got an amazing vocabulary," Chad told Jill. In the confines of his sports car, he could smell the tang of sunshine on her skin, mixed with a hint of sunscreen. "I have the impression he hasn't started kindergarten yet. Why not?''

"My mother wanted to start him in September,'' she

said. "But he'd become very clingy since, well, since his life changed."

"I'm not clingy!" Spike announced.

"You've been doing better," she told him. "And it's all right, Spike. I'm not criticizing you, just explaining things to the doctor."

"To Chad," he corrected. "I'm not here in my official capacity."

With a teasing glance, she amended, "I was just explaining things to our inconsiderate neighbor, the one with the obnoxious dogs and a habit of leaving the gate unlatched."

Chad groaned. "Can you go back to referring to me as 'the doctor'?"

"Okay," Jill chirped. "You persuaded me."

They ate at a soup-and-salad buffet restaurant where Spike helped himself to muffins and pizza-bread until Chad feared he might burst. Jill chose a salad with low-fat dressing, vegetable soup and a bran muffin. Chad, who had a plate of linguini with pesto sauce and two helpings of clam chowder, wondered how she could eat so daintily.

She must have noticed him studying her plate, because, while her nephew was getting more food, she said, "I'm not a fanatic about nutrition, but I am trying to instill good eating habits in Spike. His Dad was diabetic, which means he could have inherited a predisposition."

"Good diet may keep a person from getting adult-onset diabetes, but it won't prevent the juvenile variety," Chad pointed out.

"Every little bit counts," she said.

He supposed she was right. Still, he noted, "Studies show that keeping too tight a rein on children's eating makes them rebel. They make up for it when they're away from home.''

''I'm not a tyrant. You'll notice I'm letting him stuff himself tonight,'' she said. ''Thanks for the tip, though, Doc.''

''Maybe I could cook for you sometime,'' he said impulsively, and then wondered if he had lost his mind.

''You cook?'' she asked.

''Does Chuck Yaeger fly airplanes?''

''Yes.''

''Can Meryl Streep act?''

''Yes.''

''Well, good for them. Because I can act and maybe even fly airplanes better than I can cook,'' he said. ''Let me put it this way. Why don't you come over and watch me destroy my kitchen sometime?''

''Sounds like fun.''

Spike returned with a chocolate muffin covered with frozen yogurt. ''Look what I got for dessert!''

Chad had to wonder if the kid wasn't overdoing it. ''Maybe you could share that with me, partner.''

The boy frowned at his plate before nodding. ''Yeah, I guess it is more than I can eat.''

A few bites later Chad said, ''I can't make good on the cooking offer just yet, but I'm giving a housewarming party tomorrow—3 p.m. onward. Why don't you guys join us?''

''Please, please, please, Aunt Jill?''

''Considering that we'll probably be hearing the noise all evening, we might as well,'' she said. ''But only for a little while.''

Chad made a mental note to shop for something nutritious at the supermarket in the morning. He wondered what kind of health food went with hot dogs, hamburgers and potato chips.

JILL DIDN'T WANT TO DEPEND on anyone, ever again. Yet she found herself grateful for this man's strength.

She and Shelly together could have subdued Aaron on the bridge. At least, she thought they could have, if they'd coordinated their efforts.

But it had been immensely reassuring when Chad marched up the ladder and confronted him. It wasn't a question of macho swagger so much as quiet confidence and solid presence.

On the drive back home she watched the doctor's lean face break into a grin, revealing a small dimple in one cheek, as he and Spike discussed how to keep the dogs out of the way during tomorrow's party. He was good for the boy. A kid needed a mother, but he needed a father, too.

She nearly choked. A father? She must be suffering from post-traumatic stress disorder, or something.

Spike was describing in detail a cartoon he'd watched on television that morning. Jill was glad he'd enjoyed the show, but she thought of Chad's earlier query about why he wasn't attending kindergarten.

Yvette read to him and took him to the La Habra Children's Museum, but that was the extent of their educational activities. A quick learner like Spike deserved more intellectual stimulation than he was receiving.

"You know," Jill said during a break in the recitation, "maybe you're ready for some new challenges, Spike. The doctor might know of a good preschool around here."

"Oh, yuck!" protested the little boy.

"My nurse sends her daughter to the Flora Vista Early Learning Center," Chad told her. "It's near the mall."

"That's perfect! I work right there," Jill said.

"I don't want to go!" Spike's voice quavered. "Please don't make me! I want to stay with Yvette."

"You ran away from her," she reminded him.

"I won't do it again," he said tearfully.

Jill didn't want to force the issue. It might be best to give her nephew time to think about the idea. "We won't make any changes right away."

Chad stopped the car in front of her house. "Would it be all right if I read Spike a bedtime story?"

"Sure, if you want to." She'd expected that he would be eager to go do whatever single men did in the evening—play video games, watch an R-rated movie, work out at a gym. But apparently not.

Flicking on the living room lights, she received loud complaints from Neurotic and some plaintive meows from Normal. "It's past their dinnertime," she explained, and hurried into the kitchen to feed them.

When she returned, she found Spike giving the doctor a tour. "This is Aunt Jill's crystal vase that I must never, never, never touch. She doesn't even put water in it because it cost so much. And this thing with silver balls sticking out is a sculpture, even though it doesn't look like one, and I'm not allowed to play with it. But you're a grown-up so maybe you could push the balls and see if they make a noise."

She couldn't help laughing, although his recitation put her in a less than flattering light. "I furnished my house before I knew I'd have a five-year-old living in it. There's a den where he can play, though."

"Except I can't put my feet on the glass coffee table in there," Spike said. "Can I?"

"You won't lead a deprived childhood because you're not allowed to put your feet on the coffee table," Jill said.

Chad smiled. "I can see you both have had to make adjustments. So, partner, where's your room? Let's pick out a book."

"I've got lots!" he crowed. "But I have to put my pajamas on first."

"Don't let me stop you."

The little boy scampered off. Alone in the living room with Chad, Jill noticed how, amid the cream-colored decor with its accents of lavender, peach and rose, the man made a splash of vivid color. Navy slacks, off-white sweater, sun-highlighted brown hair, tanned skin. In contrast to his masculine proportions, her vases and sculptures looked impossibly fragile.

Maybe what she needed were posters of rock stars in their underwear. Or a poster of Chad Markham in *his* underwear. Or, best of all, Chad Markham in person, wearing nothing but a tight-fitting pair of jockey shorts that displayed his sculpted chest, narrow waistline and tight, inviting thighs....

"I'd love to know what's running through your mind," he said. "You've had the most fascinating expressions fleet across your face, one after another."

Jill's cheeks heated. One of the worst things about having a pale complexion was that she blushed deeply. "That's—that's a very suggestive sculpture you're handling," she said, meaning to joke but realizing too late that he might think she was making a naughty reference to the silver, well, objects.

"Is it?" His eyebrows lifted. "I didn't realize you were so easily embarrassed."

Her entire face must be red by now. "Could we censor this conversation and move on to something else?"

"You're not going to tell me what you were thinking?"

"No."

"At least you're honest. So where does your nephew keep his books?"

"In his room. That way."

As they walked down the hall, she heard Spike running the water in the bathroom. She guided Chad directly toward the open door to the boy's room.

Jill's mother had shipped the child's furniture and toys en masse from San Francisco. Although there hadn't been time to put up appropriate wallpaper, you could hardly see the walls anyway because of a large armoire full of toys and a tall set of bookshelves.

Chad regarded the volumes with delight. Jill had to admit, she'd been amazed by her brother and sister-in-law's many acquisitions, which ranged from the classics to picture books to interactive books that talked and played music.

"Some of my favorites!" Chad said. "*David and the Phoenix, The Phantom Tollbooth, The Runaway Bunny, Superfudge,* and the Harry Potter books."

Jill didn't have to do math to figure out he was too old to have grown up with the latter. "How did you come to read the Harry Potter books? Don't tell me they're considered medical texts."

"Only in a wizards' school of medicine." His jaw worked as he stared at the bookcase. "The truth is, I enjoy reading to children," he said at last.

"Random children you meet in the street?"

"Some of my friends have children," he said.

Was there one particular friend? she wondered, but knew she had no right to ask. "It's kind of you to pay attention to other people's kids."

"The truth is, it's self-indulgence." After selecting a Beverly Cleary book, he sat on the edge of the bed. "My parents hardly ever used to read to me. I had a series of au pairs, some of whom barely spoke English. Others were more interested in partying than in taking care of a child."

She sat in a rocking chair on which some of the Peter Rabbit stencils had worn away. Leah, her late sister-in-law, must have rocked Spike in it when he was a baby.

"Where were your parents while these au pairs were raising you?" she asked.

"Working. Dad was a surgeon." Chad's expression grew sober. "My mother's an English professor. She was often away giving lectures or traveling to do research."

"Surely your parents weren't gone *all* the time," she said. "You must have had some family occasions."

"We celebrated major holidays, usually at other people's houses," he said. "Rarely at home. I didn't even get birthday parties."

"Why not?" She couldn't believe his parents would deprive a child of some kind of recognition of the event.

"My birthday's the day before Christmas Eve," he said. "They told me there was too much going on, and they'd give me an extra present on the holiday. Which they did. Usually a gift certificate."

He sounded regretful rather than bitter. "You're not angry with them?"

"I accept that they were the best parents they knew how to be," he said. "Lots of men aren't much different from my dad. Usually the mother tries to compensate, but my mom's heart was in books and libraries and history, especially the Victorian period. That's when children were supposed to be seen and not heard."

"Are they still living?" Jill asked.

"My father died a year and a half ago," he said. "He basically worked himself to death. Six months later my mother moved to England. She'd always wanted to live there and she couldn't wait to immerse herself in her research. To tell the truth I don't think either of them should have had children."

"But you're great with kids," she pointed out.

"I'm trying to be the parent I never had." He looked up as Spike came into the room. "Hey, how about this book?" He held up *The Mouse and the Motorcycle* by Beverly Cleary.

"I haven't read that one." Spike gathered a couple of stuffed animals and climbed into bed.

"Let's give it a try." Removing his shoes, Chad sat next to the boy and stretched his legs along the mattress.

They looked so right sitting there together that Jill's heart squeezed. She enjoyed the sound of Chad's deep voice, filling the room with excitement as he read the story of the mouse who loved to ride.

This was the kind of scene she'd imagined when she was pregnant. Gary had been looking forward to having a child, and she'd pictured her sometimes-distant husband warming as he settled into family life.

Maybe he would have, although she doubted it. In any case, the pregnancy had gone terribly wrong and so had everything else.

Spike's eyelids drooped, and he buried his nose in his favorite teddy bear's fur. After putting down the book, Chad swung his legs off the bed and arranged the covers over the little boy.

He and Jill walked quietly out of the room. In the front of the house she said, "He feels comfortable with you. I think it's good for him to be around a man."

"It's good for me to be around him, too." Chad's face glowed. "Not that I'm in any hurry, but I'm looking forward to having children of my own someday. I think I'll have a lot to give them." Jill's chest tightened until she could hardly breathe. She had to look away.

There was nothing wrong with what he'd said. In fact, it was endearing.

But it felt like a slap in the face. This man, who had so many of the qualities she'd nearly despaired of finding, wanted the one thing in life that she couldn't give him.

Children.

When she first met Chad, she'd been certain he was the wrong man for her. Today she'd begun to believe there was a possibility he might be the right one.

And he might have been, under other circumstances. But although she'd worked hard to accept her losses in life, this was one she hadn't yet become resigned to.

"Thanks for reading to him," she managed to say before the silence lengthened awkwardly. "And in spite of everything, the boat ride was a good experience."

"I'll look forward to seeing you at the housewarming tomorrow.'' He lingered near the front door, studying her.

Jill held back. She didn't want him to kiss her. She wanted as little contact with this man as possible. "I'm not sure…''

"I'm stocking lots of ice cream for Spike,'' he said. "What do you eat at parties? Whole-wheat rolls, vegetables and fruit—how'm I doing?''

"Pretty well.'' She could feel herself yielding already. What could it hurt to meet more of his friends and take a dip in his whirlpool bath? Besides, Spike would insist on going.

"Three o'clock,'' he said, and went out the door before she could demur.

Chapter Five

Chad could hear the dogs growling and complaining in the garage as he finished hanging the dachshund banner from his front porch. The CD changer was loaded, the grill heating and Vic's beer chilling in the refrigerator.

This housewarming party meant more to him than he cared to let on. Or, rather, owning a house and being able to share it with his friends meant a lot.

His parents had owned a house, too, but it had never felt hospitable. Maybe it was because the clutter of objects, from the heavy furniture to the thousands of research books, left little room to move about. Mostly it was because the house served as a stopping-off point rather than an emotional center.

Chad hadn't bought much furniture yet, just the basics. But this was a place where he hoped people would feel welcome.

After putting away the ladder, he went into the kitchen to review his preparations. He'd bought a ton of food, and several friends had volunteered to bring more, so no one would go hungry. He'd piled towels next to the whirlpool bath and put up a sign that said: "Anyone caught skinny dipping will be subject to medical experiments."

He'd invited co-workers, old friends and his immediate neighbors, as well. But the one he most looked forward to seeing was the silver-blonde who'd dominated his restless dreams last night.

What was it about Jill that haunted his mind? Chad wondered. There was a vulnerability about her that touched him, yet an underlying strength, too. Underneath her wary exterior, Chad sensed vibrancy and energy. They could have a lot of fun together.

Her husband must have been an incredible jerk. He'd made her mistrustful of men, which was probably why she'd nearly changed her mind last night about attending the housewarming.

Plus, this past year she'd lost her brother and unexpectedly gained a child. Experiencing such major life changes would make anyone cautious.

In front of the house a vehicle screeched to a halt. Through the curtain-free front window, he saw Vic and Cara each grab an armful of grocery bags from the back seat and head for the front door.

"Gourmet potato chips, a world-class assortment!" Vic announced when Chad admitted him. A dark-blue bruise on the internist's forehead showed where he'd bumped it yesterday. "Ranch flavor, barbecue flavor, cheddar cheese and sour cream and onion. I've got some dip in here, too."

"I'm making a fruit plate." Cara plowed past him toward the kitchen. "Do you have such a thing as a serving platter around here?"

"We could tape some paper plates together," Chad offered.

"Didn't your mother make sure your kitchen was remotely civilized?" returned the young woman, rummaging through the cabinets and frowning at their emptiness.

"My mother isn't the domestic type." The only cooking he could recall her doing was scrambling eggs, heating canned soup and making Scottish scones from a nineteenth century recipe so she could describe the taste accurately in an article.

Vic thumped his sack onto the counter. "How cold is it?"

Chad peered through the window at the thermometer he'd posted outside. "Seventy-seven degrees."

"Not the air! The beer!"

"Check the fridge." Leaving his friend to find his own drink, he went onto the patio to make sure the ice hadn't melted in the coolers. He'd stocked plenty of sodas and fruit juices. After yesterday's experience with Aaron, who was most definitely not invited today, Chad had no interest in drinking anything stronger than Mountain Dew.

Although there was no good reason to do so, he crossed the lawn and stared over the vine-entwined fence. This morning he'd heard Jill's and Spike's voices floating upward, but by the time he got dressed they'd gone inside. Now he could see that they must have been smoothing out the displaced chunks of lawn and removing dead flowers.

Some gaping holes remained in the beds. Maybe people would bring flowering plants to the housewarming, Chad hoped. He would sneak into her yard and plant them tomorrow as a surprise.

"So where are Torero and Blitz?" Vic demanded, coming outside. "They didn't get over the fence, did they?"

Chad retreated to the patio. "They're in the garage,

but they got through the gate the other day and tore up Jill's yard. Didn't you ever train those dogs?''

Vic's jaw dropped in mock horror. ''And impose my human values on their free animal spirits?'' Helpfully he added, ''The community center has a dog obedience class on Tuesday nights. I always meant to go to it.''

''I'll check it out.'' The doorbell, which he'd temporarily hooked to a loudspeaker, rang in the rear yard. ''Guests!''

He hoped it would be Jill and Spike, but it was another medical school colleague who worked at the clinic, obstetrician Norma Chen. Six months pregnant, she had brought her radiologist husband and a basket of dried fruit.

The next arrival wasn't Jill, either. Nor the next, nor the one after that.

He hoped she would get here soon, before he was forced to do something drastic.

JILL AND SPIKE ATE LUNCH at her mother's house in Costa Mesa. Nita fixed meatballs, which she knew her grandson loved, along with salad and whole-wheat pasta in a mushroom tomato sauce.

They dined in her sunny breakfast room, on woven place mats around a blond wooden table. Nita filled them in on her charity work.

''Donations are up for the food bank, but so is demand as we get into the holiday season.'' She patted the corner of her mouth with a napkin. ''By the way, are you cooking Thanksgiving dinner or am I?''

Startled, Jill realized it wasn't an unreasonable question, although she'd never cooked a complete holiday meal before. ''I guess I am. Spike should get used to having Thanksgiving in his own home.''

"What time shall we eat?"

"Around five o'clock?"

"That's fine," Nita said. "Don't worry if I'm a few minutes late. I'll be serving early meals at the rescue kitchen. What time are you planning to put the turkey in the oven?"

Jill wished she had a tennis racket to parry the onslaught of questions. "Mom! I don't know. How long does it take to cook one of those birds?"

"That depends on the size," said her mother. "And whether you stuff it. Four or five hours, I guess."

"Can I buy a bird already cooked?"

"I'm sure you can," she said.

Jill recalled seeing a sign at the local supermarket about ordering holiday meals. She wanted to fix the side dishes herself, but not having to deal with the turkey would be a relief. "Who else should we invite?"

"That neighbor of yours who baby-sits," her mother said.

"Yvette? Of course."

"Dr. Chad!" said Spike.

"Definitely," said Nita.

Bad idea. Jill tried to come up with some convincing arguments against it, and failed. "Maybe."

Spike downed another meatball. "What time is Dr. Chad's party today? I can't wait!"

"He invited you to a party?" Nita's blue eyes met hers. "You didn't tell me."

"He invited everybody," Jill said. "It's a house-warming."

"And we went sailing yesterday," Spike put in. "I threw up, and he gave me ice cream."

"Sailing? This is getting better and better." Nita

eyed the empty dishes. Recognizing her mother's signal, Jill began clearing.

"It was okay," she said cautiously.

"And he took us out to dinner and came home and read me a book," Spike said. "Can he do that again tonight, Mom?" He didn't realize he'd called her by the wrong name, and Jill, touched, didn't correct him.

"I'm afraid he'll be busy with the party."

"So you like him?" Nita said.

"Don't get your hopes up. He wants to have children." She scraped the dishes and stacked them in the sink. Her mother preferred to load the dishwasher herself. No one else, she always complained, did it properly.

"You could adopt," her mother suggested.

"I *am* adopting," she said. "I'm sure he meant kids of his own."

"Did you tell him?"

"Tell him what?" asked Spike.

Jill glared her mother into silence. Anything spoken in Spike's presence was likely to be broadcast to the immediate world.

"You're the only child I want," she said. "You get all my attention. Now, I'll bet there's a yogurt pop hiding in the refrigerator."

There was, and it distracted Spike. It didn't distract Nita, though.

She made sure they left in plenty of time to go to the party.

CHAD DIDN'T SEE JILL ARRIVE. Someone else must have let her inside while he was making toy swords out of balloons, a trick he'd mastered to reassure his young patients.

Suddenly Spike appeared among the small group of other children who'd accompanied their parents. "Wow! Could you make me one?"

"I'd be delighted." Chad reached for another balloon.

"You're good at that." Jill appeared behind her nephew. "We should hire you at the mall."

"The man who taught me is a real master," Chad said. "He makes fantastic animals, multicolored balloon hats, centerpieces, you name it."

She was wearing, he noticed, a short, fuzzy, lavender sweater that barely met the waistband of her purple skirt. Whenever she raised her arms, a tantalizing glimpse of bare skin appeared at the waistline.

Chad forced himself to look away. That was how he happened to notice that a couple of other men were giving Jill the once-over.

He was sure they couldn't help noticing the way the sweater clung to her rounded breasts, or how slender her legs were beneath the business-length hemline of her skirt. He couldn't blame them for ogling her, but it was a good thing he wasn't in the habit of punching out rivals, or several of his guests would have been sporting shiners.

Whoa! You're turning into a caveman here.

He definitely felt protective. That was why he stuck close to Jill, making sure she was introduced around and helping her find the diet sodas.

Then Vic demanded to be relieved at the grill, and Chad had to go flip burgers. He kept an eye on Jill until he burned one burger and dropped a slice of cheese on a hot dog by mistake. He decided he'd better pay attention to what he was doing.

THE PRETTIEST WOMAN at the party, in Jill's opinion, was Chad's nurse, Cynthia Pringle. Tall and slim, with high cheekbones and dark curly hair, the African-American woman seemed to slip naturally into the role of hostess. She directed people to the bathroom to change for the pool and helped others find their drinks.

Jill was determined not to get jealous. She reminded herself that Cynthia worked with Chad every day. If there were sparks between the two of them, they would have raged into a forest fire by now.

"Your nephew is adorable," said Cynthia. "I saw him at the clinic on Friday." The nurse indicated a cute dark-skinned girl who was showing Spike her doll. "That's my Alicia. They seem to be hitting it off."

"Is your husband here?" Jill asked.

"My ex-husband? He's long gone. That's my boy-friend, Rod." Cynthia indicated a handsome man play-ing an abbreviated game of croquet with a group of people. The lawn was rather small, so they kept hitting the wooden balls into the bushes.

"He has a nice smile," Jill said.

Cynthia cocked her head and assessed Rod as if she'd never noticed his smile before. "You're right. I guess I'll keep him. So tell me, how long have you known Chad?"

"Since Friday," Jill said.

"Really? I got the impression earlier that you two had known each other for a while," she said. "In fact, I figured you must be dating, considering the way he was guarding you from the competition."

"What competition?" Jill asked. "I didn't notice any."

"He was very effective," Cynthia said. "Believe me, I've worked with that man for a year, and I've seen a lot of women make a play for him, but I've never seen him act possessive toward any of them.''

The comment warmed Jill, but she told herself that Cynthia might have misinterpreted Chad's actions. "He probably figured I need extra help since I don't know many people here. Besides, he's not exactly wilting on the vine."

The nurse followed her gaze to the grill, where Chad stood flipping burgers. Three women had gathered around him, their gazes fixed on his face.

Jill particularly noticed one small, dark-haired woman who was giggling and flirting. Her minuscule bikini showed off a figure worthy of a men's magazine.

That was the kind of girlfriend a swinging bachelor needed, she thought with a pang. The woman looked ready to fly to Las Vegas or jump onto a sailboat at a moment's notice.

Chad, however, kept his attention on his work. When a little girl came over to get a hot dog, he provided it with a flourish.

"He loves kids," Cynthia said. "You'd be surprised how many pediatricians don't."

"He's mentioned he wants to have children of his own." Realizing the nurse might misunderstand, Jill added, "It came up in general conversation."

The other woman pursed her lips. "That must have been some general conversation!"

"But he hasn't met the right woman yet," Jill added quickly. She knew it wouldn't be her, but she couldn't help hoping it wasn't anyone quite so vivacious, or so curvaceous, as the brunette in the bikini. "You wouldn't happen to know who that woman is, would you?"

"That's Susie Nunez, our receptionist." From the

nearby refreshment table, the nurse scooped some bean dip onto a chip. "Attractive, isn't she?"

"Every inch of her," Jill said.

Cynthia laughed. "She's relentlessly young and she has perfect skin. It took me a few weeks to get over the green-eyed monster when she was hired. After a while you start thinking of her as an overgrown kid."

The way Susie tilted her face and studied Chad, she didn't remind Jill of a kid. "I'd say she has a crush on the good doctor."

"Probably, but it isn't getting her anywhere," the nurse said. "She's been batting her eyes at him for six months. I think she's on her third pair of false eyelashes, to tell you the truth."

Jill's tension drained away. Not that she'd been jealous, but he deserved someone more mature than Susie.

"You know, you never answered my question," Cynthia said. "Now that I've answered yours about Susie, I'd say you owe me."

"What question?" Jill asked.

"Whether you two are dating. Since Friday, I mean."

"No." Honesty forced her to add, "We did go sailing yesterday with his friend Vic, but that was because my nephew wanted to go."

"You didn't want to?"

"I had my reservations."

"Good for you!" Cynthia said.

"Why do you say that?"

"I'm glad you're not falling all over him," she said. "Doctors get way too much ego stroking. Take him down a peg. Keep him guessing. It's good for him."

Jill wanted to deny that she had any romantic interest

in Chad, except that it wasn't true. Of course she'd be interested, if things were different.

But they weren't.

She was spared the need to reply when an Asian woman who looked about six or seven months pregnant pounced on the bean dip. "Oh, good! Fiber!"

"Norma, have you met Jill Rutledge, Chad's neighbor?" Cynthia asked.

The woman extended a hand and shook briskly. "It's lovely to meet you."

Norma Chen, Jill soon learned, was an obstetrician at the clinic. She was having her first baby and admitted that, despite her expertise, she suffered the same worries as any other mother-to-be.

"People forget that doctors get high blood pressure and morning sickness and swollen ankles, too," the woman explained. "Some days I don't think I can stand on my feet and perform another examination. Then I remind myself that this is what I've always wanted to do."

"What's your line of work, Jill?" Cynthia asked.

While Jill was explaining about being assistant marketing director at the mall, Chad joined them. Apparently, he'd run out of customers at the grill.

"What exactly does the marketing department do?" Norma asked, her eyes shining with interest. Considering that the obstetrician participated in the miracle of birth nearly every day, it surprised Jill that she would be so interested in mere merchandising.

"Quite a variety of things," she said. "We put together catalogs and mailers, stage fashion shows and supervise holiday decorations and promotions. We not only reach out to customers, we help attract new retailers and act as a liaison with the city of Flora Vista."

"What's your educational background?" Chad's deep voice sent a shiver down her spine.

"I got my degree in fashion merchandising and minored in marketing," Jill said.

"Did you always want to work at a mall?" Norma asked. "Boy, if I'd known when I was a teenager that such a job existed, I'd have gone for it!"

"You wouldn't!" Chad said.

"Well, I might have for about five minutes." She grinned. "How about you, Jill?"

"I didn't think about a mall specifically. After college my first job was at a department store," Jill said. "Then I did a stint at a public relations firm. But when I saw an ad for this job, it sounded perfect."

"And is it?" Chad asked.

"Most of the time." She and her boss had occasional disagreements, but they were minor. "I like not being tied to a desk. And being part of a community. A shopping mall's like a little city, with its tenants and customers. The general manager's like the mayor."

"How sweet!" Norma clasped her hands over her bulging midsection. "I'm taking part in your Frequent Shopper promotion. I've almost earned enough points for a gift certificate. Of course, compared to what I've already spent on maternity and baby clothes, it's a drop in the bucket."

"Listen to her!" said Cynthia. "I hear this woman had the baby shower of the decade."

From inside the house Vic wended his way onto the patio and made a beeline for Chad. The two put their heads together and then Chad said, "Jill, I need your help with something. Do you mind?"

"Of course not." She glanced around and spotted

Spike having a balloon swordfight with another little boy.

"I'll keep an eye on him," Cynthia promised.

"Thanks!"

Chad led Jill through the house and out the front door. Then she saw why he needed her help.

Standing on the curb, wearing the sourest expressions this side of a lemon-tasting contest, were Louise and Lorraine Norwalk and Sam Wright, the president of the homeowners' association.

It occurred to Jill that the trio had a reasonable gripe in that the dachshund was flapping suggestively from the top of Chad's porch. On the other hand, did they really have to interrupt him in the middle of a party to complain?

"Hi." Chad bestowed a friendly but professionally distant smile on the newcomers. "What can I do for you?"

"I'm Sam Wright." The man stood as straight as a soldier on the parade field. If Jill hadn't already heard that he was a former military man, she'd have guessed it. "I'm afraid we have a bone to pick with you, Doctor."

"Sorry about the wind sock," Chad said. "I'll take it down as soon as my guests leave. Matter of fact, I plan to donate it to a thrift store."

"I'm afraid it isn't just a matter of your banner." Sam cleared his throat uncomfortably. He was a decent enough man, in Jill's observation, but putty in the hands of the Flora Dora Girls.

"The problem is your house," Louise said.

"It's the color," said Lorraine.

"What's wrong with it?" Chad turned and studied his home.

Jill got a prickly sensation. She'd noticed when the painters were working that the background color was a bit more reddish than the hues of the surrounding houses, and the chocolate trim a bit darker. It didn't bother her, but it wasn't strictly to code.

"Didn't your real estate agent explain that you have to match the colors on our chart or else get board approval?" Sam asked.

"Match the colors?" Chad repeated. "I thought I was supposed to use them as a guideline. To stay in the ballpark."

Louise made a clucking noise. "I'm afraid you hit this one out of the ballpark, Dr. Markham."

"Well, next time it needs work, I'll make sure I hold the chart up in full sunlight and squint hard to make sure there's no digression whatsoever," Chad said.

"You don't seem to understand." Lorraine sounded almost gleeful. "You have to repaint it. Those are the rules."

"Otherwise we can fine you," Louise said. If she'd rubbed her hands together and performed an Irish jig, Jill wouldn't have been surprised.

"Is this true?" Chad asked her.

Jill nodded reluctantly. "You can read your association papers, but I'm afraid so. However, you can appeal."

Suspicion glinted in his eye. "And the people I appeal to would be the same board that's after my hide in the first place?"

"We're not after your hide, Dr. Markham," said Sam. "And there are seven members on the full board. Our next meeting is tomorrow at 7 p.m. in the clubhouse. You're welcome to make your appeal then."

Chad's jaw tightened. Jill didn't blame him for being annoyed, since repainting would cost plenty.

"Couldn't he redo the trim instead?" she asked.

The Flora Dora Girls shook their heads. Sam said, "He could mention that possibility in his appeal."

"It's been charming getting to know all of you." Chad's tone made it clear that this conversation was finished. "I'll see you tomorrow night. And possibly in court."

"You signed those papers before you closed escrow on your house," said Louise. "Courts have upheld the right of homeowners associations to impose such restrictions."

"There's no wiggle room, Doctor," added her sister.

Sam frowned at their spitefulness. "Let's not bait the doctor. Sorry about all this, Chad. It's nothing personal."

"I understand," he said, but Jill wasn't sure he did.

The three board members walked off down the street. When they were out of earshot, Chad said, "Is there a rocket to Mars leaving soon? Could I volunteer those two biddies for the honor of being among the first colonists?"

"You'd have plenty of people willing to help pay their fare," Jill said. "I'll ask Yvette to spread the word about tomorrow night's meeting. Lots of residents are sick of their meddling, and some of them might show up to support you. But other people will figure that if they have to obey the rules, so should you."

Chad jammed his hands into his pockets, which had the effect of pulling his slacks low on his hips. He looked like a teenage rebel or, perhaps, like a kid caught with his hand in the cookie jar. "It's a reasonable point, that we all have to play by the same rules. But it's not as if I painted the house chartreuse with pink polka dots."

"They're real sticklers," Jill said sadly.

"Will you be there?" he asked.

"I wouldn't miss it. I might even put in a few words on your behalf." She hated to think what nit-picking the Flora Dora Girls might engage in on her property in retaliation, but she refused to allow herself to be bullied.

As she turned to go inside, Chad touched her wrist. His hand was large and warm, and she found that she had no desire to move away.

"Most of my guests will be gone by seven or eight, since they have to be at work tomorrow," he said. "Why don't you and Spike put on your swimsuits and come back for a private soak?"

By eight o'clock Spike was likely to fall asleep on Chad's sofa, Jill realized. The two adults would be alone in the heated water, their legs tangling beneath the surface.

She couldn't think straight with him touching her. Impressions crowded her mind—of his tanned skin and smoky scent and the way his breath teased across her neck.

She hadn't been attracted to anyone since her divorce. Now this very desirable man was regarding her as if he could hardly wait to kiss her, and her breasts ached to feel his hands cup them.

She sucked in a sharp breath. "It's not a good idea."

"What just happened here?" Chad asked. "We both faded out for a minute. Were you thinking what I was thinking?"

"If I was, I'd have to slap your face," she retorted.

He chuckled. "Looks like we're on the same wavelength."

"No," she said.

"No, we're not, or no, you're not coming over for a late-night dip?"

"Both," Jill said.

His cockiness vanished. "Hey, if I'm making a pest of myself, please say so."

It bothered her to distress him. And she didn't want to alienate this man who was so good for Spike and so…so confusing for her.

"It's not a good idea for people who live next door to get too close too fast," she temporized. "Imagine how awkward it would be if we ended up hating each other."

His mouth curved with amusement. "I can't imagine that. But you're right about taking our time. I'll see you at the meeting tomorrow night, then?"

"It should be interesting," she said.

But not nearly as interesting as tonight might have been if she'd yielded to her impulses, she reflected as she went to rejoin the party.

Chapter Six

On Monday the vendor arrived to make final plans for installing the Santa Claus display in the mall's center court. Distressed at learning they'd decided to hire five Santas instead of one, he insisted it was too late to change course.

"I'm sure we could fit them in somewhere," Jill's boss, Bert, said across the conference table in his office. "Or rotate them. How about that?"

"If we don't guarantee full employment for the season, we'll never get the best quality Santa Clauses," the man replied. "It may look easy to sit around going ho-ho-ho all day, but believe me, these guys have it rough."

Jill remembered Santa's complaints from last year. "The kids spill drinks on them, and the moms set off flashbulbs in their faces."

"Bob, the guy we had last year is all signed up, anyway. We can't go back on our contract," the man added. "And he makes a wonderful Santa. The beard is real. Believe me, the way the kids pull on it, that's a big plus."

Bert went to consult Delores, the general manager. From her office, they could hear her loud reply: "I've already called a reporter from the paper about our exciting ethnic Santas. We can't back out now.''

It sounded final.

Bert had to attend a joint planning meeting with city officials, so Jill was left to play peacemaker and implement an idea she still didn't like. Finally the vendor agreed that with five Santas instead of one, the line of children would move faster, so he didn't need to allow as much waiting space.

The hastily summoned designer arrived to consult on altering the plans. He agreed that four more alcoves could be nestled among the greenery. "Although," he said, "it won't be as esthetically pleasing. Usually this mall has a top-notch exhibit, and this is going to look jammed together.''

Jill made a helpless gesture. "You're telling me.''

"I'll have to get cracking on hiring these four other guys if you expect them to be in place by next Monday," the vendor said. It was the mall's tradition—recent tradition, anyway—for Santa to arrive at the start of Thanksgiving week.

"Don't forget Mrs. Claus," she said.

"We'll have Marcia again. She's good at handing out the milk and cookies, and she loves sitting in when Santa takes a break," he said.

"Is that equal treatment?" Jill asked worriedly, although there'd been no objections last year from Marcia, a rotund grandmother who liked to earn extra money during the holidays.

"As long as she gets paid the same, she doesn't seem to care," the vendor told her.

"Excuse me," said the designer. "We need to take a look at what happens to the crowd movement when we restructure the Santa arrangement. The fire department's going to be on our case if people can't get out in a hurry.''

It was two o'clock before Jill had time to grab a sandwich at her desk. She spent the rest of the afternoon helping the third member of the marketing staff, marketplace manager Rose Rodgers, at the concierge desk across from the center court.

Rose, who had returned to work when her children were in high school, welcomed the assistance amid the chaotic swirl of shoppers. Jill helped her organize the receipts and paperwork for the mall gift certificates, the charity poinsettia sales and the Frequent Shopper program.

''We'll be starting the security escort service right after Thanksgiving,'' she reminded Rose. The mall offered shoppers a free guard on request to help them carry their packages to their cars.

''That was sure popular last year, especially among our older customers.'' Rose, who was in her early forties, broke off to direct a customer to the ladies' room. ''I'm going to provide an even better service. I'm banning my daughter from the parking lot until she gets a little more driving experience.''

''Where's she going to practice?'' Jill asked in mock alarm.

''In the middle of the desert, if I have anything to say about it,'' Rose grumped. ''That girl thinks the most important piece of automotive equipment is the CD player. I can't believe my husband bought her a car, even if it is ten years old.''

Jill tried to imagine what Spike would be like when he learned to drive, and failed. How did a single mom control a teenager who was likely to be bigger than she was? It would help to have a husband, but lots of women managed without one, and so would she.

After such a hectic day, it wasn't until she reached the gates of Terrace Crest Estates that she remembered about tonight's homeowners meeting. She also hoped Spike hadn't run away if he got bored at Yvette's.

But he was ready and waiting at her neighbor's front door, snuggling his teddy bear and ready to be hugged. "We went to the park! There was a whole group of kids. I met a little boy named Matt and he's really nice. Alicia was there, too."

"Wonderful." While cuddling him, Jill peered over his head at Yvette. "Did you reach many people about the meeting?"

"Half a dozen said they'd show up," replied the sweet-faced woman. "My back's hurting, and I don't think I can bear sitting in one of those miserable folding chairs. Why don't I come over and watch Spike for you? No charge. Besides, that way you won't be too distracted to give the Flora Dora Girls a piece of your mind."

"Thanks," Jill said. "I hope you feel better."

Yvette stretched. "I guess chasing a kid around is more strenuous than I expected. But I enjoy it!"

As Jill walked home with Spike, she wondered why she felt so nervous about the board meeting. No one was going to shoot her for speaking up and, realistically, Louise and Lorraine couldn't target her unless she was guilty of an infraction.

Then it hit her. She'd never seen Chad when she didn't have Spike along. She needed some kind of shield against him.

Is that how I'm using my nephew? she wondered. *As a way to keep sexy men at a distance?*

Until a month ago she'd gone everywhere by herself, Jill noted. She could handle Chad without any help. Still, her nerves remained on edge.

She took Spike inside, fed the cats and began fixing a dinner of soup, bran muffins and salad. Through the window she noticed that something seemed out of place in the garden.

It took a moment, in the fading light, for her to figure out what it was. The holes dug by Chad's dogs had been plugged with flowers. Odd-looking flowers.

Orchid-like cyclamen, which needed filtered light, and azaleas, which required acidic soil, had been stuck right into the flowerbed where they were sure to die. A tall clump of chrysanthemums filled a gap in the border, a spot that cried out for shorter flowers. She recalled seeing those chrysanthemums yesterday, in a decorated pot presented to Chad by one of his guests.

Staring out the window, Jill began to giggle.

"What's so funny?" Spike asked.

"We've got a hit-and-run gardener," she said, and lifted him so he could see. "Where do you suppose those flowers came from?"

"Maybe the cat planted them," he said.

CHAD WASN'T SURE what to expect from a homeowners' association meeting. Was it formal, like a city council meeting? Crowded? Noisy? Did people get angry and throw things at each other?

Whatever he'd expected, it wasn't anything quite this casual. About twenty folding chairs had been set up in the association's clubhouse, facing a table around which were arranged seven chairs for the board. The handful of people who'd arrived before him looked like retirees and, despite the cool weather, most wore shorts.

As residents trickled in, each collected a one-page agenda from the front table. There were two other items, Chad saw, the renewal of a maintenance contract for the grounds and the replacement of some worn-out playground equipment. Item number three was "consideration of member violation of paint color rules." In other words, him.

Louise and Lorraine, avoiding his gaze, took seats at the front table. Sam Wright entered and gave Chad a small nod, which he returned. He tried to assess the moods of the other four board members as they arrived.

One man looked to be in his thirties, another in his forties. Both wore business suits and had probably come straight from work. He assumed they'd be reasonable, but not particularly warmhearted.

A red-haired woman in an expensive suit and pumps dropped her leather briefcase on the table in a manner that made Chad guess she might be a lawyer. At the end of the table a sharp-faced woman in a sweat suit had soccer mom written all over her. They both looked like no-nonsense types, too.

Chad couldn't expect to find any sympathy among this batch. He'd have to hope that common sense would sway them.

By 6:55 the chairs were almost filled. There was no sign of Jill.

Maybe she'd had to work late. Or Spike might have balked at sitting through the meeting. Even though he understood there could be plenty of things keeping her away, Chad missed her.

She'd been right, that neighbors shouldn't get involved with each other too quickly. Already, he realized, he'd been counting on her support, as if the two of them were close friends.

Or more than friends. The minute he got home from work, he'd sneaked into her yard and planted the flowers received as housewarming gifts. He'd stuck them into the ground willy-nilly and fled when he heard her car pull into the garage. He'd acted like a snub-nosed kid trying to impress a girl in pigtails.

The problem was he kept wanting to go back. To spend time hanging around her, to read to Spike again, to check out the contents of her refrigerator. To make himself at home.

He had a home. Even if he had—mind you, he wasn't conceding anything—possibly painted it the wrong colors.

Then he saw her, standing in the doorway trying to spot an empty seat. Chad raised his hand to catch her attention, and indicated the seat next to him.

She angled along the row and slipped into place as the meeting was called to order. She smelled like a bran muffin, he decided.

The first two items on the agenda were dispatched quickly. Then the board came to item three.

Sam Wright held up the all-too-familiar chart of bland beiges and tans. "It seems a new resident, Dr. Chad Markham, who's here with us tonight, mistakenly believed these were only examples and painted his house a few shades too dark."

"Not only too dark, but too red," said Louise Norwalk.

"And the trim!" Her sister shook her chestnut curls as if describing a transgression that threatened civilization as we know it. "It's dark-chocolate. We had this discussion before, most of you will remember, when the Smith family made a special request for chocolate trim. We turned them down.''

"Dr. Markham has offered to redo the trim if we'll allow him to leave the main color until it needs repainting," Sam said. "Perhaps he'd like to say a few words on his own behalf."

Chad uncoiled from his chair, warning himself to keep a grip on his runaway mouth. If he went purely by instinct, he would declare that a man's home was his castle, and rules be damned.

Looking around the room at the skeptical faces of the mostly over-forty residents, he doubted he'd get much backing for such a stand. And he understood why not. No one had forced him to buy a home in a development with such tight standards.

"I'm not advocating scrapping the rules," he said. "I'm not sure I'd have bought a home here if my neighbors had painted their houses pink and green. But I made a good-faith effort to stay inside the guidelines. It wasn't clear to me that I had to match those colors exactly, although I'll certainly do so in the future. But it's going to cost over a thousand dollars for a full repaint job, and I'm asking the board to be reasonable." He sat down.

"Anyone else care to comment?" Sam asked.

One gray-haired lady stood up. "I drove past the doctor's house today. It is a little brighter than the others but if he tones down the trim, I think it could work."

After her, a portly man arose. "Maybe we all perceive colors differently, but I'd say that house isn't just reddish, it's practically bright scarlet. I say, repaint!"

Chad caught Jill's slight shrug. Apparently she'd expected reactions like this.

When no one else spoke, she stood. "I live right behind Dr. Markham and I don't object to the colors. Can we assume that all the board members have driven by the house?" Seven heads bobbed. "I'd like to hear what each of you thinks, aside from the three who've already spoken." She sat down.

Was that her big defense? Chad felt a small twitch of disgruntlement, but reminded himself that perhaps she was doing the best she could.

One at a time the other four board members spoke. Three of them conceded that they wouldn't have noticed the paint job if it hadn't been pointed out to them. The fourth considered it slightly too dark, but didn't sound disturbed about it.

Jill had been right to insist that each of them speak. "So does that mean you're going to give me a break?" Chad asked.

"Just because they didn't notice it before, doesn't mean they don't have to enforce the rules!" Louise flared.

"What's the effect going to be if one of your neighbors puts his house up for sale?" demanded Lorraine.

The two launched into a speech about real estate values that made Jill yawn behind her hand. On the board, however, other members nodded.

With no further discussion, they voted five to two to require Chad to repaint the entire house. The Norwalk sisters beamed.

Chad knew he ought to accept defeat gracefully. But it wasn't in his nature.

He got to his feet. "I have a question. Do the paint standards apply to the interior of the house?"

Several board members frowned. "This has never come up before," said the lady with the briefcase.

Lorraine Norwalk's nostrils flared. "You don't have curtains on your living room windows, as I recall. A person can see right into your front room."

"No, I don't believe the color restrictions apply to the interior," Sam said.

"So I could paint my living room psychedelic orange if I want to?" he said. "Thank you." He sat down.

Beside him, Jill uttered a noise somewhere between a groan and a chuckle. "Don't do it!" she whispered. "They'll get you one way or another."

"At least they'll be too busy to pick on that nice lady with the shade house," he murmured back.

"We can't let him get away with this!" Louise fretted. "If the walls can be seen from the street they have to be the right color!"

A murmur of protest ran through the audience. Another woman spoke up. "My living room is blue. Does that mean I'm in trouble if I leave my curtains open?"

A young man added his voice. "Hey, you can see into my garage through those little decorative windows in the door, and it's slate-gray. Do I have to repaint that?"

"It looks like you've opened a whole new can of worms," Jill said to Chad.

"Good!"

"Our rules don't cover interior paint," said the woman board member in the sweat suit. "I've got wallpaper in my front room, and I'm not taking it down every time I get my curtains cleaned."

"If there are no further items, this meeting is adjourned," Sam said.

Chad felt a flush of triumph. It abated only when he

remembered that he was still going to have to spend a lot of money making his house look boring.

"YOU HAVE TO LIVE WITH IT, you know," Jill told Chad as they left the clubhouse. Overhead, celestial lights pricked the blue-black sky.

"Live with what?" He grinned in a boyish way that made her want to hug him, or maybe spank him.

"An orange living room, if you paint it that way." In the thin light from a streetlamp, she made her way along the sidewalk. Since she lived a mere three blocks from the clubhouse and the night was mild, Jill hadn't brought her car.

"I don't have to paint all the walls orange," he said, matching her stride. Apparently he hadn't brought his car, either. "Only the one facing the street."

"You're unbelievable. Tell me, when do you plan to grow up?"

"Do you need a definitive answer on that?" he asked. "I'm in no hurry."

"There's no reason you should be." Jill had to admit she'd enjoyed watching him thumb his nose at the Flora Dora Girls, even though he'd lost. "I guess this is what they call a moral victory, isn't it?"

They waited on the curb while a car went by, then crossed a small residential street. "An expensive moral victory." Chad shuddered. "Not to mention that I'll have to move out while they paint. The fumes give me headaches."

"Only if they paint the interior, right?" she said.

"I'm not backing down. And you shouldn't want me to."

"I don't. Not really," Jill admitted. "I do hope you're not setting a bad example for Spike."

Chad mulled her point over before answering. They passed one- and two-story stucco houses that, even at night, had a solid, prosperous air. "I'll explain to him I'm not taking the law into my own hands. I'm standing up to tyranny."

"Of a minor, if annoying, sort." Her athletic shoes slapped against the pavement as they crossed another street.

"Most tyrants take your freedom a little at a time, so it never seems like a big deal," he said. "Besides, I get the feeling Louise and Lorraine wouldn't have objected so strongly to my paint if I hadn't stood up for your neighbor in the first place. That's what bothers me most, that they're vindictive."

"I agree," Jill said, "and that's why I'm not going to bandy about words like *adolescent* and *beneath you.*"

He stopped on the sidewalk, threw back his head and laughed. The moonlight gleamed off his throat and highlighted the strong thrust of his jaw.

From a bush in the adjacent greenbelt drifted the scent of jasmine. Another half block and they would separate to walk to their own houses. Jill wished they could linger for a while longer.

Perhaps Chad was wishing the same thing. Instead of resuming their walk, he indicated a gazebo set back on the greenbelt. It looked summery and welcoming in the silver light. "Who owns this?"

"We do," Jill said. "It's community property."

"It reminds me of the Victorian era." Turning from the sidewalk, he covered the short walkway in a few steps and entered the circular pavilion. "That gazebo roof over the whirlpool was one of the first things that drew me to my house."

Jill reminded herself that she should hurry home to relieve Yvette. But she didn't really want to go. Not yet.

She followed him into the quaint little structure. There was nothing wrong with enjoying a man's company for a few minutes.

And she did enjoy his company. Not only his conversation, but his silences, as well. His presence filled the space as he leaned on a railing, staring into the starry night.

"Which one's Sirius, the Dog Star?" he asked.

"The brightest one," Jill said.

He pointed. "There?"

"That's a satellite," she said. "You'll notice that it's moving."

"I figured it was unruly, like my two dogs," he said. "By the way, I called to inquire about obedience classes, but the new session doesn't start until January."

"Better late than never. Oh, thank you for planting the flowers in my garden." She decided not to mention that he'd put them in the wrong places. She would quietly move them next weekend, the cyclamen to her front planter and the azalea to the side yard.

"You're welcome." Even across a gap of several feet, his nearness enveloped her.

Jill tried to think of something else to say. Something about Spike. Or flowers. Or rear gates.

She couldn't think of anything except the warmth radiating from Chad as he shifted closer. He was a perfect height for her, tall enough to be commanding but not too tall for her arms to drape easily around his shoulders as he pulled her against him.

Her face tilted upward, and their mouths met. A tingle ran through her lips and across the points where her body measured his.

His fingers stroked the back of her neck, and his hand cradled her head. A sweet sense of languor crept over Jill. She experienced Chad with a slowly spreading sense of pleasure.

His mouth hardened against hers, his tongue probing. Her tingling sensations intensified into sparkles, and when his hips pressed against hers, a flame licked deep within.

The laziness vanished. Long-suppressed desire shook her with its sudden urgency. Jill had to force herself to pull away.

Chad let her go reluctantly. They stood motionless in the cooling air, both breathing fast.

"I didn't plan this," he said.

"I know," she murmured. "It was as much my fault as yours."

"Fault?" His lips twisted into a lopsided grin. "You make it sound as if we did something wrong."

"I...I don't know what I meant," Jill admitted. "Or what I want. Or what you want."

"Shall we have an intense philosophical discussion, or can we just enjoy the moment?" he teased.

She wanted to enjoy a lot of moments with him, but Jill knew she'd be playing with fire. She didn't dare invest so much of herself in a relationship with a bachelor who, she guessed, probably changed girlfriends often. And who, if he wanted a wife, needed one who could give him children.

"I still don't think it's a good idea for neighbors to get involved," she said. "We live too close."

"But imagine the possibilities!" Moonlight glinted off his merry eyes. "We could sneak through the back gate to meet each other at night, and frighten the pixies in the garden.''

"More likely we'd scare the heck out of my cat," she said. "She's neurotic enough already."

"I don't suppose there's any point in inviting you over for a drink?" he asked.

"Yvette's baby-sitting, and she needs to rest," Jill said. "Her back's giving her trouble."

"It's as good an excuse as any to go home and not finish what we started."

A lump lodged in her throat. Did the man have to read her mind so accurately? "Okay, you've pegged me for a coward. Well, you're right."

"I like challenges," Chad said. "And I like you."

"There'll be other challenges." Jill tried to keep her tone light. "I'm sure one will come along any minute."

"I don't know what your ex-husband did to you, but I'm not him," he told her. "My attention span lasts a lot longer than that."

"I'll look forward to finding out exactly who you are, then," she said. "I just don't want to move too fast."

It sounded like an invitation, Jill noticed. She'd left the door between them open wider than she intended.

"I'll be around," Chad said. "I'm not going anywhere, except to Las Vegas this weekend."

"In case I don't see you before then, enjoy yourself."

"Will you miss me?"

"It'll give me time to move the flowers around without you noticing," she shot back.

"I thought they looked a little funny where I stuck them," he said affably. "I'll come take a look on Monday. Maybe it'll teach me something about gardening."

And he walked off toward his house, whistling. He'd scored as many points off her as he had off the Flora Dora Girls, Jill decided.

She hated to admit how much she was looking forward to a rematch.

Chapter Seven

During the next few days, Spike asked several times when they were going to see Chad again. Jill had to tell him she didn't know.

After their kiss in the gazebo, she'd wondered if he would drop by later in the week, but he didn't. He must have taken her at her word, that she didn't want to move too fast.

At least, she hoped that was the explanation.

On Saturday she worked at the mall, overseeing the construction of the Santa Claus set. Her mother took a delighted Spike to an amusement park.

Jill was glad no one asked whether she'd invited the doctor for Thanksgiving dinner next week. She'd decided not to. It seemed too personal, at this point, to have him meet her family and take part in such a special occasion.

One thing she'd learned, the first year after her divorce, was that sharing so many holidays with Gary had, at least temporarily, tainted them. That postdivorce Christmas prickled with his memories, and the Fourth of July stung with the recollection of previous holidays spent watching fireworks from his boat. She didn't want next Thanksgiving to be filled with the memories of Chad if he failed to stick around.

Nevertheless it was a relief to see the lights flick on at his house on Sunday night, and to hear the happy yelps of his dogs, which he must have picked up at a kennel. Jill didn't know what he'd done in Las Vegas or who, besides Vic, had gone with him, and she didn't want to know. She was just inexplicably glad to see that he was home, even at a distance.

At the mall on Monday she forgot her personal concerns when the Santa Clauses arrived. All five of them, plus Mrs. Claus.

Bob, the Santa from last year, frowned on seeing the others. "What's going on?"

"Didn't anyone tell you?" Jill, to whom had fallen the duty of installing everyone, got a sinking sensation. Without waiting for an answer, she said, "We're trying something new this year. Five different ethnicities of St. Nick."

"You're kidding," said the rotund, red-faced man. He was so perfect for his role that she had a hard time imagining he lived anywhere other than the North Pole and worked at anything other than supervising toy-making elves.

"Are there five Mrs. Clauses, too?" asked Marcia, a grandmotherly figure who'd brought home-baked cookies to share with the staff.

"No. I guess the other Santas are bachelors," Jill said.

"Or I'm a polygamist," Marcia replied cheerfully. "I should have brought more cookies."

They were standing at the center court with an hour to spare before the shops opened. The other four Santas, already in costume, wandered toward them.

They were of differing heights and builds, and none looked comfortable in fake white whiskers. "Hi." She extended her hand to an African-American man. "I'm Jill Rutledge, assistant director of marketing.

"I'm Rafe Adams," he said.

"Is this your first gig as Santa?"

"I did it last year in Compton," he said. "But I didn't have competition."

"We're trying something new," Jill explained.

"So I heard."

She introduced herself to Santa José, Santa Wong and Santa Whitefeather. Although friendly toward her, they eyed each other dubiously.

"I'm not sure how to say ho-ho-ho," confided Santa Wong, who was making his debut in the role. "Do you kind of shout it—Ho! Ho! Ho!—or chuckle, hohoho?"

"Like this." Santa Bob gave out a cheery, gut-busting rendition that brought waves of laughter from senior citizens participating in an early-morning exercise program.

"Let's figure out who sits where," Jill said. It was going to be a long day, she could tell.

THAT AFTERNOON no one answered the doorbell at Yvette's. Anxiously Jill banged on the door, but still received no response.

Had she and Spike gone out? It wasn't like her neighbor to plan activities late in the day.

Suppose Yvette had fallen ill. Suppose...

Sternly she got a grip on herself and turned the knob, which opened easily. Why had the door been left unlocked?

Her heart thumping, Jill stepped inside. "Yvette? Are you here?"

She made her way through a living room jammed with curio cabinets and china knickknacks. It really wasn't geared for an active child like Spike, she conceded.

Initially she had been more concerned about his sense of security than about his schooling, and had decided that a one-on-one caretaker would be ideal. Now she wondered whether she'd made the right decision.

A TV set murmured in the rear den. Jill hurried to reach it, only to find the room empty. Through the glass door she scanned the backyard with no luck.

Calling Yvette's name, she checked the bedrooms. Jill had never been in this part of the house before, and it took a minute to locate the master bedroom.

Inside, the last rays of daylight played over a form lying on the bed. After one anxious moment Jill saw the woman's chest rise and fall evenly. Apparently Yvette had fallen asleep.

If only Spike were also taking a nap. But a glance at the covers dispelled that notion.

"Yvette, are you all right?" Jill touched her neighbor's shoulder. "Where's Spike?"

The woman blinked awake. "What? Oh!" She sat up, frowning. "I took some pain medication for my back. What time is it?"

"After five," Jill said.

"That was two hours ago." Yvette's eyes widened in alarm. "Oh, my gosh. Spike's missing?"

"He must have gone out the front door." Jill tried to think clearly. Last time he'd headed for the clinic. And all this week he'd been asking about Chad. "I have an idea where he might have gone."

"I'm so sorry," Yvette said. "I let you down."

"You were trying to help." Jill knew her neighbor

had offered to baby-sit more for Spike's sake than because she needed the income. "But it might be best if I look into finding a preschool. You need to rest your back."

"I'll watch him until you find one," her neighbor promised. "No more pain medication on duty, either."

"Not the kind that makes you sleepy, anyway." Jill sighed. "I'll call you when I find him."

She was halfway out the front door when she spotted Chad's red sports car stopping at the curb. The passenger door opened and Spike jumped out.

"Never mind," Jill called back to Yvette. "He's here!"

"Thank goodness," the woman said from within the house. "Give him a scolding for me. And a hug, too."

"See you tomorrow." Jill strode out to the sidewalk and was greeted by her nephew, who waved a lollipop.

"Look what Chad gave me!" he said.

Jill knelt to hug him. "No ice cream this time?"

An amused male voice responded. "I didn't want to reward him for running away."

She straightened, and tried not to show how glad she was to see Chad. He looked carelessly handsome in the fading light, his brown hair rumpled from a busy day and his white coat creased. "Thanks for bringing him home."

"Alicia's mom said to say hi," Spike added.

Jill was momentarily at a loss as to who Alicia might be, let alone her mother. Then she remembered the nurse and the little girl from the party. "We ought to get you two kids together to play."

"As a matter of fact, she asked me to give you this." Chad handed over a business card. It bore the name

Flora Vista Early Learning Center. "If he went there, they could play together every day."

"That would be fun, wouldn't it?" Jill asked Spike.

His little face grew shadowed. "I like Aunt Yvette's. Even if she did go to sleep."

"Maybe we could take a look at it," Jill said.

"How about now?" Chad asked. "Then we can try out a Chinese buffet restaurant I spotted."

"Only if you let me pay," Jill said. "To thank you for bringing him home."

Chad's gray-green gaze explored her face. Was he as aware as she that a whole week had passed since they'd seen each other? Had he, too, relived their kiss, cherishing it, feeling the fires spark all over again?

Jill swallowed. She shouldn't allow herself to fantasize. The man had plenty of other things on his mind, and so did she.

"I'll let you pay," he said, "this once."

"Let's go." She shooed Spike into the back seat.

CHAD WAS RIDICULOUSLY GRATEFUL for an excuse to have her in his car again. Especially this snug little sports car, where his arm brushed her thigh every time he changed gears.

Las Vegas, with its circus acts and amusement themes, hadn't been nearly enough of a distraction. Everywhere Chad had caught himself searching for a tumble of silver-blond hair and the sweetly wary face of a grown-up angel.

He was trying to give her the space she needed, and to slow down his own headlong tumble into an involvement that might not be in his best interest. Jill was a complicated woman, and hadn't he vowed to simplify his life?

Yet the sight of her sent his hormonal system into high gear and his spirits into the stratosphere. After eight hours spent tending to kids with runny noses, ear infections and harassed mothers, the last thing he should have wanted was to inspect a day-care center, and yet he was looking forward to it, as long as he was with Jill.

Across from the mall, the Early Learning Center sat slightly below the street. Chad noted approvingly the large, walled play yard with imaginative equipment and a shock-absorbing surface.

When they entered the lobby of the blue-and-yellow building, they heard only a few children's voices. At a quarter to six, most of the youngsters must have gone home. The posted closing time was only fifteen minutes away.

The director, Mrs. Sanchez, bustled out and welcomed them, despite their lack of an appointment. Chad, who had belatedly remembered to remove his white coat, was taken for the father until he identified himself as a family friend.

When they entered the large playroom, Chad waved to a gap-toothed little boy. "There's Matt! I met him at the park."

Alicia must have left already, but the remaining children were happily pretending to cook dinner on a play stove. Mrs. Sanchez explained the daily program, which included a story hour, learning colors, shapes and numbers, activities to develop motor skills and a reasonable amount of free play.

By the time they left, he could see that Jill was sold. Spike grumbled and clung to her hand. Still, he kept wiggling around to wave to his friend.

At the Chinese restaurant, they piled their plates with

food. Spike selected plain rice, teriyaki sticks and, to Chad's surprise, broccoli.

"He likes it," Jill explained when they sat down. She'd chosen sparingly, as usual.

Chad wondered how she mustered the self-control to deny herself so many goodies, then remembered that she was concerned about developing diabetes like her late brother. He supposed that someday he'd start worrying about heart attacks and cut back on his own take-no-holds approach to eating. Not for a few years, though.

"Are you going to repaint your house?" she asked.

"Do I have a choice?"

"You could drag your heels and make life difficult," she said. "It's been done in the development before."

"I prefer to take my lumps and move on." Chad plowed into a mound of beef and vegetables. When he came up for air, he said, "I called the painters for an estimate. They said it's their slow season and offered a discount, so I'm having the work done in two weeks."

"Inside, too?" she asked.

"One wall in the living room." The paint smell would be enough to drive him out of the house, but he couldn't very well suggest moving in with her, much as he might want to. "So, not to change the subject, where are you going for Thanksgiving?"

Jill hesitated with her fork in midair. "Uh...family," she said vaguely.

"You can come, too!" Spike said. "Aunt Jill's cooking a turkey."

"Spike!" she said.

"Well, you are," he replied. "I heard you talking to Grandma Nita."

Chad coughed and weighed tactics as he swallowed some water. He didn't want to take unfair advantage of the boy's offer to eat Thanksgiving dinner with them. Correction: he did want to take advantage of it but he didn't want to seem pushy.

He settled on an apparently neutral remark. "That should be a sight to see." *Okay, now invite me to watch.*

"I'm not really going to cook a turkey." Jill wedged some hair behind one ear. "I'm going to buy it already cooked."

"Good idea. No mess to clean up. Except the one in your dining room, of course." *Translation: are you eating at your house? Because if you are, it would be cruel not to ask me to come.*

"Yvette's baking pies, and Grandma Nita's making the salad and the fruit salad," Spike mumbled through a mouthful of rice.

"Yvette bakes? I'm impressed." *Gee, you included one neighbor. Why not make it two?*

"You've probably already got plans," Jill said.

She's weakening. "Not really."

She stared at her fork, which had stopped in midair. *Okay, here it comes.* "Of course you're welcome to join us."

"What time?" Chad asked.

"We're meeting at four, eating at five."

"What can I bring?" He had a pantry stuffed with leftover potato chips and a refrigerator full of aging potato salad. Neither of those was likely to suit. "Rolls?" He'd heard of something called brown-and-serve rolls, which sounded right up his alley. "And ice cream. Gotta have ice cream."

"Yes!" said Spike.

"That would be fine," said Jill.

By TUESDAY she stopped kicking herself and accepted the fact that she'd been backed into a corner. She couldn't have rescinded Spike's invitation without acting downright rude.

Besides, she didn't want Chad to languish alone on Thanksgiving. With his father dead and his mother living in England, he didn't have relatives to turn to, and she doubted his friend Vic was planning anything so domestic.

It was going to be awkward, but she tried not to dwell on that. She did her best to act pleasantly distant on Tuesday evening when Chad dropped by on the pretext of observing how she'd replanted the flowers.

He listened gravely as Jill took him around the yard and explained why and where she'd moved everything. She doubted he retained a single word. He kept staring at her lips and taking her arm to help her over imaginary rough places in the lawn.

It had been an unreasonably long time since she'd had a man's arms around her. Being near Chad stirred longings that took on a life of their own. It was a relief when he left a few minutes later, and a disappointment, too.

That night Jill dreamed of tangling in the sheets with him. Of sweaty golden skin and demanding hips pressing against hers. Of a sweet, aching surrender and the lovely glow that followed.

But there was pain connected with the dream, or the memory, or whatever it was. The glow faded to loneliness, and the man went away, leaving an emptiness far greater than the one he'd filled.

On the way to work Wednesday, Jill dropped off a completed application at the day-care center. Mrs. Sanchez assured her that Spike could start on Monday morning and would fit in well. "He's a bright little boy," she said. "He's been through a lot, but children are resilient."

Jill wished grown-ups were equally resilient.

She parked in an outlying spot and walked across the mostly empty pavement into the mall. Some senior citizens from the Dawn Patrol of early-morning mall exercisers greeted her en route to her office.

"What's with the five Santas?" asked a woman.

Jill explained that it was an experiment.

"Dumb idea," said a man. "This is carrying political correctness to extremes."

"I think it's nice," said the woman.

"There's a reporter coming today from the newspaper," Jill said. "Apparently this is unique."

"Let's hope it doesn't catch on," grumbled the man. Silently she agreed with him.

The past two days had been crazy as she'd helped sort out the lines of children and repeated her explanations to their skeptical parents. As a result she was backlogged on her other work. She needed to hire strolling musicians for the holidays and get copy ready for the mall's advertising agency.

An unmarked door near the concierge desk admitted Jill to a long, narrow corridor. She walked past doors labeled with the names of adjacent shops and through a larger door bearing the notation Mall Offices.

In the waiting area milled half a dozen people—customers, judging by their casual clothing. It was rare to have so many visitors, especially at this early hour.

"They want to talk to someone." Across the counter the receptionist clasped her hands nervously. "Delores isn't here yet, and Bert's out walking the mall. He's not answering his cell phone.''

''Walking the mall'' meant he was refilling racks with promotional magazines, changing out-of-date announcements and looking for graffiti or missing signs. Bert had an uncanny knack for not being around when unpleasantness hit, Jill thought, and chided herself for being uncharitable.

With an inward straightening of the spine, she stated her name and title. ''Now, how can I help you folks?''

A man stepped forward. ''I'm Fred Riley, and we want you to stop this nonsense with the five Santa Clauses.''

''It's confusing our children,'' a woman said. ''My little girl's asking if Santa really exists and, if so, which one is he?''

A Hispanic woman folded her arms. ''It's good to celebrate diversity, but this doesn't seem to me to be the best way.''

''My wife's so upset she's threatening to shop somewhere else this Christmas,'' added a man.

''I'm open to suggestions, but we've already hired the Santas,'' Jill said. ''We thought about rotating them, but their contracts call for full-time work.''

''Do you mean you'd change the arrangement if we can give you a good alternative?'' asked the first man, Fred.

''It's not up to me, but I'll be happy to plead your case with our general manager,'' Jill said. ''Our goal is to please our customers, not antagonize them.''

The outer door opened. She was hoping to see Bert or Delores but instead in came a young man with a camera slung over his shoulder and a notepad in his hand.

The reporter! He wasn't due for another half hour. When he saw the crowd, he brightened the way Spike did when someone offered him ice cream.

"Lou Meany from the *Flora Vista Journal*," he said. "It looks like we've got a controversy on our hands. Somebody fill me in, will you?"

The customers weren't shy about repeating their beefs, in even more aggravated tones than before. By the time the general manager showed up ten minutes later, Lou Meany had nearly filled his pad.

FOR THE REST OF THE DAY complaints flooded in. There were also a few calls of congratulations from community leaders, who told the mall staff not to back down.

"I want you all to think about this over the Thanksgiving weekend," Delores said at a hurriedly called staff meeting. "Bert and Jill, talk to people on your shifts, and then on Monday we'll discuss what to do."

The Santas, of course, would be working Friday, Saturday and Sunday, which were among the busiest shopping days of the year. Jill wasn't looking forward to her Friday shift, even though she loved the excitement of the holiday season.

"I feel so bad for everybody," she said. "The kids are asking questions their parents can't answer, the parents are cranky, and the Santas seem to feel they have to compete with each other."

Today, Santa José had brought candies to reward children for choosing his lap. Santa Bob was ho-hohoing louder than usual, and Santa Whitefeather's family had come in Native American clothing to show support and warmly greet his line of youngsters.

"You have to admit you're not objective," Bert

pointed out. "You didn't like the idea in the first place."

"That doesn't make her wrong," Delores said. "Let's put on our thinking caps over the weekend."

Who has time to think? Jill wondered as she left later that afternoon. She had to stop at the supermarket to buy ingredients for the Thanksgiving dishes she'd be cooking and to order a turkey for tomorrow.

"I'm sorry, but precooked turkeys had to be ordered by Monday," the deli clerk told her.

"What?" Jill stared, disbelieving. "But you cook them tonight, right? And you've got a store full of turkeys."

"We roast them at a central location," the woman said. "The arrangements had to be made in advance so they could have enough birds on hand."

Jill spent the next quarter hour on her cell phone, calling other supermarkets and a couple of restaurants with no luck. Finally she gave up and bought a fresh turkey, which had cooking instructions printed on the wrapper.

"It's cheaper, anyway," she consoled herself between gritted teeth.

When Jill got home, a beeping sound alerted her to a message on her answering machine.

It was from her late brother's lawyer in San Francisco. The man, Ben Nyman, wanted Jill to call him as soon as possible. If she couldn't reach him today, he urged her to try again after 9 a.m. on Monday.

It was six o'clock. The phone at the law office rang a dozen times before she hung up.

What could he have been calling about? Whatever it was, she hoped it wouldn't delay the adoption.

The cats needed to be fed, and she had to collect Spike. Resolutely Jill put the call out of her mind.

Chapter Eight

Flora Vista Medical Clinic was closed on major holidays, except for a pediatric walk-in clinic. Chad had volunteered for the 7 a.m. to 3 p.m. shift on Thanksgiving.

Every parent who came in made a similar remark. It went something like, "Wouldn't you know it? They always get sick on holidays."

"Germs and accidents don't take vacations," was nurse Cynthia's standard response. For his part Chad would merely nod and continue his examination.

He especially liked the little children clutching dolls and teddy bears. Sometimes the older kids brought stuffed animals, too. Teary but brave, they endured poking and prodding and sometimes shots.

His most serious case of the day was a broken arm incurred while performing unsupervised gymnastics. He referred the girl to a hospital for X-rays.

There was a subdued air at the clinic, compared to most days, he noticed as he prepared to leave. The staff joked less than usual, and no one lingered at the end of a shift. Everyone was in a hurry to join family and friends.

Last year, soon after he'd arrived in Flora Vista,

Chad had deliberately worked the late shift so he wouldn't mind so much that he had nowhere to go. The year before that, at the inner-city hospital, he'd taken one of the nurses, Marie, and her three children out to dinner, but it had been a subdued affair since she'd learned that her abusive ex-husband would be released from prison soon.

Come to think of it, he realized as he got into his car, he didn't have many fond memories of Thanksgiving. His father, a cardiologist, had often been called to the hospital for emergencies. His mother, who was indifferent to any holiday that hadn't been celebrated in Victorian England, generally forgot to shop in advance and cooked whatever she could thaw out.

She had a theory that chicken was as good as turkey. Chad supposed she was right objectively, but there was nothing objective about Thanksgiving.

He'd always envied the kids on TV, whose extended families sat around a big table heaped with special foods. In college he'd eaten at a friend's home once and been overwhelmed by the delicious smells and the warmth among the people gathered there. The next year, he'd volunteered at a soup kitchen, but the loneliness of the clients only intensified his own isolation.

Today was different. Today he was going to Jill's house.

Chad had to restrain himself from whistling as he stopped at an open supermarket. Two packages of brown-and-serve rolls ought to be enough. He added a gallon of vanilla ice cream to go with Yvette's pies and a gallon of chocolate-fudge ice cream for pigging out.

He got into the spirit so much that he responded with interest when the elderly woman in the checkout line ahead of him began to chat. Chad agreed with her that, my goodness, those models on the magazine covers wore less clothing every year, and could you believe it was almost time to start Christmas shopping?

Christmas shopping. The words reminded him that he would need to get a couple of rubber bones for the dogs. A few things for Cynthia and her daughter, maybe a book for Spike and something special for Jill.

He wished he knew a gift that would banish the wariness from her face and make her smile as if she had not a care in the world. A gift that would send her flying into his arms and make the rest of the world disappear while her wonderful, soft breasts rubbed against his chest....

"Excuse me...I said, will that be all, sir?" asked the checkout clerk.

"I'm sorry," he blurted. "I was thinking about sex."

"Me, too," said the man behind him.

"It's those magazine covers," muttered the clerk, and made change for Chad's twenty-dollar bill.

JILL HAD NEVER REALIZED there were so many ways to cook a turkey, and each claimed to be the only right way. The turkey wrapping said to cover with foil, then remove the foil for browning when the bird was almost done. An Internet site instructed her to put the turkey inside a plastic bag. At an 800 number she called, the recording insisted she baste repeatedly and cover the skin with foil only if it got too burned.

"What do you think?" she asked Neurotic.

The cat's look said, *Skip this nonsense and feed the whole thing to me.*

"You can eat the giblets when they're cooked," Jill replied. Then she had a horrifying thought. Giblets reminded her of giblet gravy. She needed to make gravy and she had no idea how.

"I'm calling Mom," she said.

No one answered. Nita must have already left for the rescue mission. Quashing a spurt of annoyance, Jill dug out a cookbook and found a recipe.

She was going to master this turkey and gravy business. The fact that Chad would be eating here had nothing to do with her determination to succeed. Well, very little, anyway.

As she tucked the turkey into the preheated oven—foil and plastic free, since she'd decided to go with basting—she wondered if he'd ever had a girlfriend who cooked Thanksgiving dinner for him. Probably lots of them. A cute, energetic guy like Chad must draw women like flies.

Yet from time to time she caught a hint of loneliness in his expression. He'd obviously loved reading to Spike and being part of a family....

A family. Jill's chest squeezed. To Chad, and to most men, having a family meant having children that were genetically descended from them. That was certainly what it had meant to Gary.

Not to Jill, though, yet she still mourned the baby she'd lost at eight weeks' gestation. Spike had made all the difference. She'd bonded quickly with her new son, and maybe, if she met the right man, they could adopt another child, as well.

But that was asking a lot. Why would a man choose to marry a woman who couldn't have children?

Jill smacked the cookbook onto the counter and turned to a recipe for brown rice and lentils. Just because it was Thanksgiving, that didn't mean she couldn't fix healthy food. Or think healthy thoughts, ones that had as little to do with Chad Markham as possible.

JILL SET THE DINING ROOM TABLE with the china and crystal left over from her long-ago storybook marriage to Gary. He hadn't argued about her keeping the silverware, place settings and linens when they divorced. After all, he had plenty of money.

He'd remarried last year, she'd read in the newspaper. His new wife was a computer executive from out of state, so perhaps they'd met at a convention. Although Jill told herself she didn't care, she was glad he hadn't married his former assistant—the woman he'd cheated with while still married to her.

No doubt the young woman had foolishly believed he loved her, when he'd only been trying to prove his manhood. Or to punish Jill in some twisted way. She didn't envy his new wife, that was for sure. Gary wasn't a guy who stuck around when the going got tough.

Was Chad? She visualized him storming up to the top of the boat to confront the drunken Aaron. That had taken courage.

On the other hand he spent his spare time gambling in Las Vegas and throwing parties. That wasn't the lifestyle of a man who expected to settle down anytime soon.

"Can I help?" Spike's eager face appeared at her elbow.

"Sure. Pick out five forks, spoons and knives, and I'll show you where to put them."

He counted the silverware and listened attentively to the correct order for setting. The pieces went on the tablecloth a bit crookedly, but Jill was sure no one would mind.

The timer buzzed. She darted into the kitchen, grabbed the potholders and took out the turkey.

Crisp and golden-brown, it sported a few pieces of protective foil atop the wing points. The thermometer in the stuffing showed 165 degrees and the one in the meat read 180 degrees.

"I guess that's done." She set the roasting pan on top of the range to cool. "Now I have to drain the juices to make gravy. Boy, is this complicated."

"I'm done setting the table!" Spike announced. "What else can I do?"

The bell rang. "You could answer the door." Jill debated removing the apron from over her blouse and skirt, but decided she'd rather appear frumpy than gravy splattered.

It was Yvette, bearing pies. She insisted on taking over the gravy making, much to Jill's relief. A few minutes later Nita arrived with a salad, fruit salad and homemade orange-cranberry sauce.

Spike gave them each a hug and lingered by the front window, watching for Chad. Jill's heart tugged as she observed him.

He'd grown attached to their neighbor. She hoped it was only a reaction to missing his own father and that in time he wouldn't feel so needy. When Chad moved on to other interests, she didn't want her little boy to get hurt.

She didn't realize how intently she was listening until the doorbell rang. Her hands fluttered at the apron strings, untying them despite her practical intentions.

"You look nice," her mother said, regarding the

V-neck blouse and the soft, swirling fabric of the skirt. "Very feminine."

"I figured it would be a nice change from business suits," Jill said as she hurried into the living room, where Spike had already opened the door.

Chad bent down to place a grocery sack in Spike's upraised arms. He towered over the tiny figure like a benevolent giant. "That's ice cream, now, so don't drop it."

"I won't," the little boy said solemnly. "Look, Mom! Two things of it!" He called her Mom more and more often now.

"Two gallons for five people? What luxury," Jill said.

"Also rolls. They need to go in the oven." Chad hoisted a second sack. "And here's your newspaper from the driveway. You forgot to bring it in."

"Thanks." She was so busy sorting out the things he handed her that she couldn't do more than sneak a sideways glance at the man. But that was enough to send her heart rate into the stratosphere.

A heather-green sweater made his eyes shine like jade. And there was pure joy in his smile, most likely a reaction to the aroma of roast turkey. She'd noticed at the Chinese restaurant how much he liked to eat.

Maybe a little of that radiance meant that he was glad to see her, too. Jill hoped so.

She made the introduction to her mother. Nita beamed at Chad. "I'll take charge of those rolls," she said. "Whole wheat! What a great choice."

"Of course. I wouldn't buy anything less." As soon as she vanished with them, he murmured to Jill, "It was dumb luck. I didn't notice what kind of rolls they were."

"You rogue!" Jill said.

"I think she knew I was joking. Don't you? Mmm, something smells good." He followed his nose into the kitchen.

Yvette exchanged greetings with her neighbor. "Too bad about the association making you repaint."

Chad explained the situation to Nita. "I've got painters coming a week from tomorrow. I'll have to move into a motel for the weekend."

"Maybe not." Nita cocked a meaningful look at her daughter. "You've got a spare bedroom, haven't you?"

"Mom!" Jill refused to be bullied. "It wouldn't look right to have a man stay here."

"Who's looking?" her mother asked.

"I would never take advantage of a neighbor's generosity," said Chad, which Jill assumed was about as truthful as claiming that he never bought any kind of rolls except whole wheat. She knew where to draw the line, however, and this was the place.

"There's a motel a block from the clinic," she said. "I'm sure you'll be comfortable."

"*Comfortable* is a relative term." Removing the lid from a casserole, he sniffed the contents appreciatively.

"He can use my room," offered Spike. "I'll sleep on the couch."

Chad had the good grace to look guilty. "I'm just teasing, sport," he said. "Your mother's right. It isn't necessary."

Since Nita and Yvette had taken over the final preparations, Jill ducked into the dining room and opened the newspaper. Subconsciously, she supposed; she'd dreaded reading what that reporter had written about the mall using a number of different Santas.

She scanned the front page and gulped. At the top was a photo of Santa Whitefeather and his family greeting a couple of youngsters. The headline read: The More the Merrier? Some Parents Say No.

It looked as if Lou Meany had lived up to his last name, she thought grimly.

Chad came to glance over her shoulder. "Trouble in Toyland?"

Jill flipped the paper over so they could read the article below the fold. It featured reactions from children, parents, customers, store owners and community leaders.

Some applauded the ethnic Santas, and others gave the mall points for trying. Overall, however, people were dismayed by the confusion.

The article concluded, "Will the real Santa Claus please slide down the chimney? We want to know what you think! Call this number to record your comments."

No doubt the responses would be printed on Monday. It meant lots of publicity for the mall, but Jill wasn't sure she agreed with the philosophy that any publicity was better than no publicity.

"Seems like a tempest in a teapot to me," Chad said.

She turned and discovered he was closer than she'd realized. So close that her cheek brushed his shoulder, and she inhaled a trace of leather-scented cologne.

Her response was immediate and physical. She hoped he didn't see how her breasts tightened beneath the thin fabric of her blouse. But the doctor had never struck her as unobservant.

"I...I hope it blows over quickly," she said.

His cheek grazed her hair. "You could divide and conquer. Put each Santa in a different part of the mall."

She forced herself to concentrate on his suggestion and not on the heat stirring within her. "We've already got historical tableaux around the mall, showing Christmas through the ages."

"Coming through!" cried Yvette, and the two of them sprang apart. Jill hadn't realized they were blocking the dining room doorway until her neighbor carted a platter of carved turkey between them.

"That looks great," Chad said.

"Very tender," Yvette confirmed.

"You beat the odds," added Nita, following with the stuffing. "Your very first turkey, and it's done to perfection."

Jill went to fetch more food. Soon they were seated amid the abundance, holding hands and saying a prayer of thanksgiving.

For this moment she put everything else out of her mind. The five Santas. The phone call from her brother's lawyer.

All that mattered were these people gathered around the table, their faces aglow. Chad looked boyishly eager, Spike wiggled in anticipation of eating and Yvette couldn't stop beaming at everyone. Although it had been a difficult year for Nita, who had lost her son, she radiated satisfaction as she surveyed her daughter and grandson.

Happiness swelled inside Jill. It was a rare, perfect moment, and she relished it.

MONDAY WAS SPIKE'S FIRST DAY at preschool. When they arrived, Jill was pleased to find his friends Matt and Alicia already busy playing with Legos. Her nephew clung to her hand for a moment and then ran to join them.

"He'll be fine," the director said. "You're doing what's best for him."

Jill had a hard time pulling herself away and trusting that her little boy would be safe in this new environment, but she knew Mrs. Sanchez was right. Spike needed the companionship of other children and the stimulation of an organized program.

As she drove across the street to the mall, she remembered that she needed to call the lawyer's office in San Francisco. It wouldn't be open for another hour, though.

Maybe he had good news. Perhaps the adoption could go more quickly than expected.

Inside the mall members of the Dawn Patrol greeted her. "Did you read the paper this morning?" "What did you think?" "Are they going to change the Santa arrangement?"

The reaction to the story of the Santas had been overwhelmingly negative. Readers hated the idea of having five St. Nicks.

One woman said it encouraged greed among children because they would demand more presents. Several people cited the value of honoring tradition. A man called it an airheaded attempt to please everyone that ended by pleasing no one.

"I don't know," Jill told the senior citizens. "We're having a meeting about it this morning."

When she reached her desk, she found a note from Bert, who'd worked the Saturday shift. The meeting would begin at 9 a.m., it said.

It looked as though that call to the lawyer would have to wait. Resignedly, Jill set down her purse and went out to walk the mall.

She arrived back to find solemn faces assembling in

the conference room. Bert and Rose Rodgers looked as if they'd just returned from a funeral. The heads of security, maintenance and housekeeping were equally grim-faced.

The general manager entered and took her position at the head of the table. "We could call it a misjudgment or we could get right to the point and call it a disaster," she said. "Now, how do we defuse the situation without firing any of the Santas?"

"We could decorate them with wild colors and turn them into an art exhibit, like the city of Chicago did with those cows they had all over the sidewalks," said the head of security, who'd always had a bizarre sense of humor. "I saw those on TV."

"They weren't live cows," Bert noted. "They were mannequins. And it was a charity fund-raiser."

"Any other suggestions?" Delores asked dryly.

"Maybe they don't all have to be Santa," said Rose. "Four of them could be elves."

"Which four?" Bert asked. "I can't see Bob as an elf, but if we make him the only Santa, we'll be discriminating."

A heavy silence fell. In the outer office, telephones rang, no doubt with more complaints about the plethora of St. Nicks.

Jill remembered Chad's suggestion about relocating the Santas around the mall. At the time she hadn't seen how it could be managed, but the notion must have been percolating in her subconscious. "It would be a lot of work, but..."

Half a dozen faces turned toward her, filled with a mixture of hope and skepticism. "But what?" said Delores.

"We could remake the historical tableaux and put a

different Santa in each one to depict Christmas around the world," she said. "They could still hold children on their laps and listen to their wish lists, but this way the parents could explain that they were representing Santa as he appears in other places."

"So they're all the same Santa," Rose said encouragingly. "Since he's magical, he could be in more than one place at a time."

"It might work," muttered Bert.

"Anyone object?" Delores asked. "We've got to do something fast. Other papers are sending their photographers this week, and I'd like to have something positive to show them."

"It's going to be a pain in the budget," said the head of maintenance.

"Unfortunately, we don't have a lot of choice," Delores said. "With luck, we can fix up the tableaux cosmetically and avoid a lot of expensive reconstruction. It won't be our finest hour, but it might satisfy all sides. Good job, Jill."

"I can call the contractor right away, if you'd like," she volunteered.

"Let's get on it," Delores said. "What else do we need to do?"

Everyone offered comments, and soon they had a workable plan. As soon as the meeting adjourned, Jill flew to the phone.

She was so busy, she didn't come up for air until nearly noon. That was when she remembered about the lawyer, and, with Bert's permission, placed the call.

His secretary put Jill on hold. Her hands got damp as she waited. She didn't want anything to delay or interfere with Spike's becoming her son.

"Ms. Rutledge? Ben Nyman here," said a male

voice on the other end of the line. The lawyer was, she recalled from meeting him once, a short, earnest man. "Thanks for returning my call."

"Is anything wrong?" She tried to keep a quaver out of her voice.

"There are two things I needed to inform you about," he said. "First, you recall that your brother left no list of assets. Since he and his wife didn't have much equity in their house, it appeared that Spike's inheritance would be small."

"Yes, I know." Jill intended to put the few thousand dollars he would receive into a college fund.

"We've learned that your brother also owned a one-third interest in his investment counseling firm," the lawyer continued. "Were you aware that they had developed a line of investment software that's being sold over the Internet?"

"No." Ellery had rarely discussed business with his sister or mother.

"The rights to the software have been sold for a considerable sum. Also, his partners have made a substantial offer to buy out his share of the company," Nyman continued. "Young Leon will receive something on the order of two million dollars."

Jill stared blankly at a Flora Vista "City of Flowers" calendar on the wall. It was almost time to flip to December, she registered distractedly as her brain struggled to absorb the news.

Two million dollars. It was such a large sum that it sounded like pie in the sky. "Is this a possibility or an actuality?"

"If the court approves the sale of assets—and I'm sure it will—the estate should be receiving the money shortly," the lawyer said.

"Who decides what's to be done with it?" That was a lot of money for a college fund. It should be invested to safeguard Spike's future, Jill thought.

"That depends on who's going to have custody of the boy," the man said. "That's the second thing I want to talk to you about."

Her stomach lurched, but surely he couldn't be implying that there was any doubt. "My mother doesn't feel she can handle raising a child," Jill said.

"There's another interested party," he said.

Another interested party? Jill's sense of disbelief intensified. "Who on earth could that be?"

"You're aware that Spike's mother, Leah, has a sister," Nyman said.

"Yes." Fiona Bainbridge, whom Jill had met a few times, was a twenty-five-year-old college dropout who lived in Berkeley and changed jobs frequently. She'd been a waitress, a cosmetics saleslady and a telephone astrology consultant. "She made it clear she had no intention of seeking custody of Spike—I mean, Leon."

"She's changed her mind," he said.

Anger charged Jill's response. "The two million dollars wouldn't have anything to do with it, would it?"

"It seems she's recently married." The lawyer didn't discount Jill's statement, she noted. He was, however, clearly trying to stay neutral. "Her husband, Geoffrey Wagner, manages a gas station in Oakland. They believe Leon would do best in a two-parent home, and she'll be giving you a call soon to arrange a visit."

Fury spurted through Jill at Fiona's gall, but she felt a pang of fear. A judge might agree that two parents were better than one. He might not see that Fiona's change of heart had more to do with dollar signs than with maternal feelings.

She couldn't give up Spike, for his sake—and her mother's and her own. Losing the boy would break everyone's heart.

"Does the adoptive parent automatically gain control of Spike's money?" she asked. "Shouldn't it be safeguarded by a trustee, such as a bank?" If Fiona couldn't get her hands on the money, she might change her mind.

"That's a possibility," the attorney said. "Once we receive the money, I could petition the court to have it put in trust. That will take a while, though."

"There's no hurry on the custody matter, is there?" she asked.

He made a sympathetic clicking sound. "Mrs. Wagner—the former Miss Bainbridge—seems in quite a hurry to 'get the boy settled in his new home,' as she put it."

Jill had to stall the woman. If Fiona took Spike now, she might find a way to grab his money, and then she'd never let him go.

"Do you think her argument, about having two parents, would convince a judge?" she asked. "Even though I've been taking care of Spike?"

"He's only been with you for, what, six weeks?" Nyman said. "And with your mother for a few months before that. Personally, I think Mrs. Wagner's chances of prevailing are at least fifty-fifty."

An idea formed in the back of Jill's mind. A crazy idea, but she was a desperate woman.

"Do your best to get that money into a trust as quickly as possible, will you?" she said. "I'll take care of Mrs. Wagner."

"Good luck," said the lawyer. He didn't sound optimistic.

Chapter Nine

"You've got that gleam in your eye," Cynthia Pringle said when she came into the staff room and found Chad eating his lunch while stretched along a fake-leather couch.

"What gleam?" he asked around the edges of a tuna sandwich.

"That I'm-up-to-something gleam," she said.

"I'm trying to figure out where to stay this weekend while my house is being painted." The idea of withering away in a motel rubbed him the wrong way. After the warmth of Thanksgiving, he wanted more.

"How about Vic's boat?" she asked.

"He's taking it out." Besides, Chad had already agreed to spend a week later in the month on a ski trip with Vic and a bunch of his buddies. The company of those rambunctious, testosterone-overloaded tomcats wore thin after a while.

"Let me guess." The nurse took a yogurt from the refrigerator. "Your girlfriend lives right behind you. You wouldn't be trying to charm your way into her house, would you?"

"Me? Take advantage of a sweet young thing?" Having finished the sandwich, he wondered what else was in the refrigerator and whether the other staff members would mind if he helped himself. Most likely they would. "Of course, I'll be working Saturday, so it's not as if I'd be underfoot all the time. And somebody's got to eat those turkey leftovers."

"This weekend will be too late for turkey leftovers." The nurse sank into an overstuffed armchair.

"Really? I save cold cuts for weeks. Months, sometimes," he said.

"Doctor! Haven't you ever heard of food poisoning?"

"Haven't you ever heard of a cast-iron stomach?" His thoughts returned to the subject at hand. "Maybe I could sprain my ankle. Injuries bring out a woman's motherly instincts."

"That's really lame. No pun intended," she said.

"Or I could circulate reports of a prowler in the neighborhood," he mused, glad for the opportunity to bounce proposals off Cynthia. "Jill might want to keep me around for protection."

"Then who's going to protect her from you?" demanded the nurse. "Most likely she'd borrow one of your dogs."

He was running out of ideas. Where was the patron saint of pathetically lonely bachelors when you needed him?

"I'll think of something," he said. "I've got until Friday."

THE FIVE SANTAS and Mrs. Claus gathered in the conference room at 4:30 p.m. on Monday. Jill had to break the news to them because Bert, who had set up the meeting, ducked out to meet with the contractor about remodeling the tableaux.

"I suppose you've guessed that there are going to be some changes," she said.

They nodded without speaking. For once even Marcia seemed at a loss for words.

Surveying their apprehensive faces, Jill couldn't help thinking of her own worries about Spike's custody. But she mustn't allow herself to dwell on personal issues at work.

"We've come up with a plan that we hope will satisfy everyone," she said. "You'll each have your own station in a different part of the mall, representing Santa around the world."

"But who's the real one?" Rafe asked.

"You all are," she said. "Santa's magic. He can be in more than one place at a time, and people see him differently in different countries."

They digested this information in silence. Then Marcia said, "Which Santa do I appear with?"

That issue hadn't been addressed. To leave her in the Center Court with Bob would be to single him out as the main Santa. He did have seniority, and got to keep his old post marked Scandinavian Santa to represent his ancestry. But that didn't entitle him to be the only one with a wife.

"We haven't decided," she said. "Perhaps you could rotate, Marcia."

Santa Wong shook his head. "I really think we should each get our own Mrs. Claus."

Heads bobbed around the table.

"Five Mrs. Clauses?" Jill said. "That isn't in the budget."

"My wife would do it for nothing," said Santa Whitefeather.

"We can't allow that." Jill sighed. "There's insurance liability and a question of fairness. She shouldn't have to work for free.''

"I sympathize, Jill, but unless you solve the Mrs. Claus problem, we're still going to have a lot of confused customers,'' Bob said.

"Not to mention a confused assistant director of marketing," she admitted. "Well, guys—and Marcia—give me a chance to think this over, will you?"

"You're not going to get rid of me, are you?" Marcia asked fearfully.

"Definitely not,'' Jill assured her. "I'm willing to entertain any other ideas you come up with, though.''

Everyone promised to think about it, and the meeting ended. Jill hurried to collect her purse.

It had been Spike's first day at the Early Learning Center. She hoped it hadn't been nearly as traumatic as her day.

WHEN CHAD ARRIVED HOME, Torero and Blitz greeted him with such gusto that they left muddy paw prints across his shirt, and he noticed that the rear lawn was beginning to resemble a battlefield. Much as he appreciated their high spirits, he was looking forward to reining in the dogs' rambunctious natures. Too bad the dog obedience class didn't start till the new year.

He would have to put the pair in a kennel this weekend to keep them from pestering the painters. They sure hated being locked away, but he didn't see how he could ask Jill to take them when it would mean having to relandscape her yard afterward—and inconvenience her cats.

Over the rear fence he noticed the black-and-white cat patrolling Jill's flower bed. She showed no fear of the dogs now that the gate was shut. Smart cat, he thought.

Chad fed the dogs and went into the house to change. After pulling off his shirt, he paused in the living room. He supposed passing motorists could see him standing there bare-chested, but he wasn't violating any association rules.

Bright-orange on the rear wall ought to do the trick, he mused, or maybe lime-green. Could he live with lime-green? Purple was too dark to show up well. Then he wondered why he hadn't chosen gold. Now, that would be truly, eye-catchingly tacky.

The doorbell rang. Chad weighed the merits of putting on his shirt, but hoped he'd get lucky and find himself half-naked in front of the Flora Dora Girls. That ought to chill their chimes.

He opened the door. Jill's blue eyes went wide, and although she returned her gaze quickly to his face, he could feel the fiery trail it had left on its expedition down his torso.

"Am I interrupting anything?" she asked.

"Come in." He stood back and, after the briefest of pauses, she entered.

The living room held very little furniture. The old couch from Chad's apartment had gone in the den, and he'd installed only one bookcase and a low end table. He couldn't even offer her a seat.

"Do you exercise in here?" she asked.

"I'm not that much of an exhibitionist," he said. "I go to my health club or use the machine in the den. In fact, you're welcome to come over and exercise anytime you want. In any room of your choosing. Alone or with company."

"That's very generous," she said dryly. "Maybe I'll invite my aerobics class."

"That wasn't the kind of company I meant." Deciding he'd reached the borderline between flirting and leering, Chad retreated to safer ground. "What would you think about gold paint?"

"I think it blocks the pores." She removed a loose tortoiseshell comb from her silver-blond hair and worked it back into place.

"Not on my body! On the wall." He indicated the blank expanse facing the windows.

"How about shocking-pink with glitter?" Her elfin chin lifted mishievously.

"Absolutely. Terrific idea." Here was his chance to remind her that he needed a place to stay while the house was full of fumes, but he couldn't imagine a good reason for her to let him occupy her guest room. Not when both of them knew it would be asking for trouble.

In fact, the longer he stood there watching her breathe in her incredibly fascinating manner, the more his usual glib banter deserted him. The only thing he could think to say was, "Where's Spike?"

"My mother took him out to eat," she said. "She wants a little grandmother-grandson bonding."

So Jill was alone this evening. And she'd chosen to come over to Chad's house. That sounded promising.

"What a rare opportunity for me to take you out to dinner," he said.

"Thanks, but I'm still eating the turkey leftovers," she said.

"Need any help?"

He'd meant it as a joke. To Chad's dismay, Jill's

expression darkened. "Not the kind of help you can give, I'm afraid."

"What kind, then?"

"Well, I—" Her lips quivered, and she swallowed hard. "I got a phone call today—" She broke off, her eyes glinting.

"Are you crying?" he asked in amazement.

"I'm...trying not to." Two fat tears rolled down her cheeks.

Forgetting his shirtless state, Chad gathered her into his arms. As she rested her cheek against his chest, he felt her shake with sobs, and experienced an overwhelming urge to pummel whoever had done this to her. "What kind of phone call?"

"About Spike. From his...lawyer." She burrowed into Chad, burying her nose in the middle of his chest as if she were trying to escape a deadly threat. "They're trying to take him away."

"Who's trying to take him away?"

"His other aunt!" Her tear-stained face lifted, and her frantic eyes met his. "His mother's sister. It turns out Spike's inheriting a lot of money, and she and her new husband claim he should have two parents. But she didn't want him before!"

A year ago Chad had vowed never again to meddle in other people's problems, particularly not problems involving women and children. But this was Jill and Spike, and he couldn't let them down.

"Come in here." He guided her through the doorway into the den and eased them both onto the overstuffed couch. "Tell me about it."

As she talked, Chad filled in the picture. This Fiona was seizing the chance to get rich, as if Spike were nothing more than a stock option. Maybe she'd persuaded herself that one aunt was as good as another, but she had to know deep inside that it wasn't true.

"She's coming Saturday!" Jill wailed. "A few minutes ago I found a message on my answering machine. She and her husband, Geoff, will be staying at that motel near your clinic. She says they want to spend time with Spike so he can 'get used' to them."

Chad's brain searched for some way to help. It didn't immediately latch on to anything. "What can I do?"

"I have an idea. That's why I came to see you." Jill fished in her pocket and found a tissue. Chad was impressed. All he ever found in his pockets was spare change and lint. "Would you mind staying at my place this weekend?"

"Excuse me?"

"You could sleep in the guest room while your house is being painted."

"Sleep at your place?" he repeated, scarcely daring to trust his ears.

"That's what I said." Her mouth quirked, but he couldn't tell if she was amused or impatient. "Twice."

"So you did." It occurred to him at this point that he might be dreaming. Perhaps he'd fallen asleep after work and fantasized this entire encounter. On the other hand, if he were fantasizing, Jill wouldn't be sitting on his couch blowing her nose into a tissue, she'd be ripping off her blouse and pulling him on top of her.

"What do you say?" she asked. "About being my houseguest?"

"I think I could see my way clear." If this was a dream, why not push his luck? "I'll have to figure out where to put the dogs, though."

"They can stay in my backyard." She tugged her skirt so it covered her knees. "I'll lock Neurotic's door so he can't leave the house. One weekend indoors won't kill him.''

She was willing to take Torero and Blitz? Now he knew he was dreaming. Or that she was desperate. ''I take it there's some fiendishly clever reason why you're willing to put up with me for the weekend?''

''I want you to pose as my fiancé,'' she said. ''I want to give Fiona the impression we're living together.''

Chad digested this information. ''What is it you hope to accomplish?''

Jill folded her hands on her lap. It was amazing how every movement highlighted the soft contours of her figure, even through her demure dove-gray suit. ''Fiona, from what I know of her, isn't very sophisticated. I don't know about her husband.''

''You think she'll back off because you suddenly claim to be engaged?'' he asked.

''I suspect she believes it's going to be easy, sweeping in here and claiming her 'dear nephew,''' Jill said. ''I'm hoping we can stall her until the money's locked into a trust where she can't get it. *Then* I bet she'll back off.''

It was a reasonable plan, and Chad didn't see how he could refuse. Staying with Jill was exactly what he wanted to do, anyway, and it might save Spike from a lifetime of misery.

On the other hand, he could find himself hip-deep in a messy situation. Custody battles had a way of spiraling out of control. Caution, and bitter experience, warned him to say no.

''Yes,'' he said.

''Yes, you'll stay at my house and yes, you'll pretend to be my fiancé?'' she asked.

''Right.'' Chad had never let caution rule his life,

and he wasn't about to start now. "What are you going to tell Spike regarding, well, everything?"

"I don't know," Jill admitted. "I'll try to explain the situation with Fiona in a way that's not too threatening. This weekend isn't going to be easy for him, but he'll enjoy having you around."

"I'll enjoy having me around, too. Around your house, I mean."

"I won't even ask you to fix the faucet in the master bathroom," Jill said. "Unless you really want to."

"I'll bring my tools," he promised.

JILL COULDN'T BELIEVE he'd agreed. She'd figured that asking the great Dr. Markham to pose as her fiancé was a crazy idea and had brought it up only because she was willing to try anything to hold Fiona at bay.

But he'd said yes. He was going to stay here all weekend, in her house, sleeping right down the hall from her.

Nothing was going to happen, she told herself. So what if, that time when they'd kissed, she'd nearly been carried away by her own response? This time she wouldn't let him close enough to strike a spark, let alone ignite a fire. Even though he was doing her a huge favor.

When she got home, she went into the spare bedroom and began clearing away the boxes, magazines and other odds and ends that had accumulated. She also stripped the covers from the bed and fetched clean sheets.

Chad wouldn't be arriving for another four days. Nevertheless, she was too energized to leave the tasks for later.

As she smoothed the sheets over the mattress, Jill

imagined his tall frame filling the room. The odors of fabric softener and lemon oil would be replaced by a musky scent with a trace of antiseptic solution and a hint of…dog.

Good heavens, had she agreed to board his dogs in her yard? She sank onto the edge of the bed and wondered if she'd lost her mind.

Letting Chad stay here was going to be risky in more ways than she'd expected. His visit would wreak havoc on her lawn and her orderly existence as well as her self-control.

She had to do it, though, for Spike's sake. Thank goodness it was only for the weekend.

WHO COULD FIGURE OUT GROWN-UPS? Spike wondered. Sometimes Aunt Jill did something smart, like inviting Dr. Chad to move in for the weekend. Then she did something kind of silly, like turning his dogs loose in the backyard.

Through the window he could see Torero eating the new pansies she'd planted. What kind of stupid dog ate flowers?

Neurotic, who had sneaked outside even though her special door was locked, sat on the back fence licking her paws. She sneered down at the dogs.

Still, the dogs weren't mean-tempered or anything. And Spike would rather spend the rest of his life watching pooches eat pansies than have to go live with an aunt he barely remembered and an uncle he didn't know at all.

It was almost time for his favorite Saturday TV show, but he didn't feel like watching it. Aunt Fiona and Uncle Geoff would be here *any minute*, as Aunt Jill kept saying in an unhappy voice.

He wondered if he could hide until they left. If they couldn't find him they couldn't make him stay with them. But Aunt Jill said they didn't have the right to take him away. And that maybe they never would.

He was glad Chad was here. Spike felt safer with the doctor nearby. He hoped the painters would move into Chad's house and make him stay here forever.

That would be best of all.

THE DOORBELL STARTLED JILL, even though she'd been expecting it for quite some time. Fiona had called last night and said she and her husband would be over at eight o'clock. It was now 8:40.

As Jill finished transferring wet laundry into the dryer, Chad appeared from the hall. "Is it okay if I put my arm around you while they're here?" he asked lazily. "How about if I call you honey-bunchkins?"

"Don't you dare!" Jill's nerves were stretched as tight as violin strings.

"Hey, relax," he said.

The doorbell rang again. Jill's heart skipped half a dozen beats. "Coming!" She skimmed toward the front room.

She'd hardly slept last night, although she didn't know whether it was due to nerves about this morning's meeting or to the knowledge that Chad was sleeping down the hall. He'd arrived with a few clothes and a ravenous appetite and taken over the house.

He seemed to be everywhere, his dynamic presence changing the air pressure, the dimensions of the rooms, even the intensity of the light. Jill couldn't concentrate on her cooking or anything else.

At bedtime he'd read to Spike and, cradling the little boy, asked about preschool. Her nephew had spilled out details about his friends and teachers that Jill had tried unsuccessfully to pry out of him.

Taking a deep breath, she opened the door.

"Jill!" Two black-rimmed brown eyes peered up at her. She'd forgotten Fiona was so short. And when had her long dark hair been cut, frizzed and dyed the colors of a rainbow?

"Fiona. It's good to see you." She managed a hug. The woman reeked of cosmetics. "This must be Geoff."

"Yo," said the toothpick-thin man beside her, flicking back a hank of shoulder-length red hair. He had a pleasant face, Jill conceded, but she wasn't crazy about the tattoos on his arms.

"Please come in." As nonchalantly as possible she added, "I'd like you to meet my fiancé, Dr. Chad Markham."

"Doctor?" Fiona blinked up at Chad as they shook hands. "Is that, like, a nickname?"

"Not really," he said.

"Yo!" Geoff shook hands, too. "This must be Leon." He indicated the little boy peering from the kitchen.

Fighting to unclench her jaw, Jill introduced the boy to the two newcomers. Spike took a step backward.

"Like, come see my pictures." Geoff indicated his tattoos. To Jill, he said, "Kids love these, you know."

"Interesting." Chad examined Geoff's upper left bicep. "Is that a mermaid?"

"It's a Lorelei," Geoff replied. "Most people don't know what a Lorelei is. Do you, Doc?"

"I'm a bit hazy on my mythology," Chad said. "Fill me in."

"It's, like, a German mermaid." Geoff, the shorter

of the two by several inches, beamed at this display of knowledge.

"Cool." Chad glanced at his watch. "I'm afraid I'm due at the clinic. I'll see you two tonight."

"Count on it," Geoff said.

Chad slipped an arm around Jill's waist. His handsome face leaned close and he brushed a kiss across her cheek. "I miss you already, sweetie-cakes," he said, loud enough for the others to hear.

She wanted to punch him.

Chad ignored her flinch. "She's a great gal," he told the Wagners. "I'm a lucky, lucky man."

"Then why haven't you given her a ring?" Fiona asked.

A ring. The words echoed frantically in Jill's mind. They'd forgotten the ring.

"I'm saving up," Chad improvised. "I want our ring to be special."

"With diamonds and rubies, huh?" The shorter woman sounded envious.

"I guess some people like that fancy stuff." Geoff shrugged. "On your way out, man, let me show you my wheels." The two exited together. From the front porch, Jill heard Fiona's husband say, "Don't you love T-birds? I restored it myself. Mint condition. Don't make an offer, though. It's not for sale."

"I can see why," came Chad's reply.

"One of these days he's going to own his own garage." To Spike, who was watching from the doorway, Fiona added, "You'll like our apartment, Leon. There's a pool and playground equipment and lots of kids."

"I like it here," Spike said.

Fiona clasped her hands, and Jill realized she was

nervous. She felt a flicker of sympathy for the younger woman, but it died instantly. "Why did you decide you wanted to adopt him now, when you showed no interest six months ago?"

"Six months ago I wasn't married," her guest replied promptly. "Do you have coffee?"

"Sure. I'm sorry. I meant to offer you some." Jill led the way into the kitchen. She reminded herself that, in spite of everything, Fiona was Leah's sister.

The two couldn't have been more different. Leah had been a teacher with conservative taste in clothes. She would never have worn the stomach-baring halter top and skin-tight, three-quarter-length pants that Fiona had on, and she probably wouldn't have chosen her younger sibling to raise her son. But since there'd been no will to name a legal guardian, Jill couldn't prove that.

She served the coffee with cookies. Spike filched a couple and stood in the corner, eating them.

Outside, the dogs sent up a loud baying as if they'd treed a small animal. Jill looked out, afraid that Neurotic was in trouble again, but they were barking at the painters working in Chad's yard.

"Are those your dogs?" Fiona asked.

"They're my fiancé's," she said.

"I didn't know you were engaged. When are you getting married?" She fiddled with her coffee cup and slopped a little on the table. "Oh, sorry."

Jill mopped it with a paper towel. At the same time she shot a glance at Spike. She'd explained that she wanted Aunt Fiona to think that Uncle Chad lived here, but she hadn't said anything about marriage. Mercifully, the little boy didn't react to the comment. "We haven't set a date. But we want Spike—Leon—to make his home with us.''

Fiona wrinkled her nose. ''You don't look like you need the money. I mean, your guy's a doctor and you've got this nice house.''

''Money has nothing to do with it,'' Jill said. ''We love him.''

The woman's chin rose stubbornly. ''So do I. He's as much my nephew as yours.''

There was no point in arguing. Jill reminded herself that she didn't expect to change Fiona's mind, merely to keep the custody issue unresolved until the money was put in trust. ''So what kind of plans do you have for the day?''

''We're taking Leon to the beach,'' Fiona said. ''Since it's nice and warm out.''

''It'll be a lot cooler at the beach,'' Jill advised. ''I'll pack his jacket, and you might want to take a sweater.''

''I can see the weather for myself,'' Fiona replied. ''Don't you think it's warm enough for the beach, Leon?''

The little boy loved digging in the sand and chasing the waves, Jill recalled from last summer. So she wasn't surprised when he nodded.

''See? He can't wait to go!'' Fiona stood as her husband came into the room. She'd barely tasted her coffee.

''You should see the sports car that doc drives,'' Geoff told his wife. ''Red as a fire engine, and it purrs like a kitten.''

''I like your car better.'' To Jill, Fiona said, ''We'll be back when you see us. Leon, go change into your swimsuit.''

''I'll put sunscreen on him.'' Jill followed her nephew. She was going to make sure he took a jacket, too, whether his other aunt liked it or not.

Chapter Ten

Vic, who got off his Saturday shift earlier than Chad, dropped by the pediatrics office on his way out. "Okay, it's going to be a little crowded week after next, but we'll have fun."

Chad looked up from reviewing a chart. "How crowded?" He'd regretted more than once agreeing to spend a week in Colorado with his buddies, but he'd put down a deposit and given his word, so he couldn't back out now. Besides, if he didn't use his remaining week of vacation before the end of the year, he'd lose it.

"There'll be six or seven of us in the cabin," Vic said. "Mostly guys."

"Mostly?" Chad knew he should expect surprises from his friend; that didn't mean he had to like them.

"Cara's coming, and Aaron's bringing Shelly..." Vic launched into a recitation of who was coming and where they'd be sleeping in a two-bedroom A-frame cabin. Chad was certain he'd get stuck either in the cramped attic or on a pullout couch in the living room.

He thought wistfully of the comfortable guest room in Jill's house. He'd slept well last night, especially considering that his male hormones could sniff out her female hormones at a hundred paces. He'd like to stick around longer, even if it meant hiring the painters to redo the rest of his house in the same electric-yellow he'd finally chosen for the living room. It seemed more cheerful than his original choice of bright orange.

Unfortunately, Jill's invitation was only good until Fiona and Geoff left. That meant he'd get the boot on Monday, and he didn't relish spending the next two weekends at home inhaling new-paint fumes.

"I'll bring my sleeping bag," he told Vic. At least that way he'd be sure of not having to share a mattress with some hairy, snoring roommate.

"'Atta boy," his friend said. "I knew I could count on you to be a good sport."

Cynthia came down the corridor with a young patient. A second glance revealed that it was Spike, struggling in vain to hide his tears.

"Hey!" Chad squatted to the boy's height. "You were supposed to be with Aunt Fiona and Uncle Geoff."

"I hate them!" The little boy threw his arms around Chad. "I want you to be my daddy!"

"That sounds like an exit line to me," said Vic. "I'll see you later."

"Later," he echoed absentmindedly before returning his attention to the boy. "What happened?"

"It was cold at the beach." Spike sniffled, and Chad handed him a tissue. "I wanted to play, anyway, but Aunt Fiona complained. So we left before I got to build a sand castle."

"Tough luck," he sympathized.

"We went to a hamburger place, and they had a neat playground." The boy blew his nose. "But she got bored, so we went to the park. It has a playground, too.''

''What about Geoff?''

''He played with me for a while, both places. Then he got tired.''

Chad caught Cynthia's signal, which reminded him that he had patients waiting. ''Where are they now?''

''Arguing. They're in the park.'' From Spike's hand gesture, Chad gathered he meant the one directly across the boulevard from the clinic. ''Geoff called Fiona a spoilsport. She said he was ruining everything.''

''How did you happen to hear this?''

''I fell off the play fort and cut my knee. So I went over to them. I…I guess I was crying.'' He showed a scrape that had a little blood oozing from it.

''They brought you here?'' Chad asked in surprise.

''No. Fiona told me to go away.'' Spike gulped. ''She said I was a crybaby.''

''You crossed that busy street by yourself?''

The boy nodded solemnly. ''Aunt Jill always washes my cuts and puts on a Band-Aid. It hurts to walk and I didn't want to go all the way home, so I came to you.''

Chad hugged the boy. ''I'll tell you what. Nurse Cynthia will take care of your cut, and you can watch TV in the waiting room till I'm done here. It'll be about twenty minutes. Okay?''

''Okay!'' Spike brightened. ''It's almost time for my second-favorite TV program.''

Chad considered calling Jill and letting her drive to the park to notify Fiona that Spike had turned up. He decided against it. The ''doting'' aunt and uncle had left a five-year-old boy essentially unsupervised in a park, even ordering him to go away after he hurt himself. Let them take the consequences of their actions for another twenty minutes.

They might learn something.

Spike didn't look happy about having to go back to the park to find Fiona. Chad held onto the boy's hand to reassure him, and after a while the boy's expression softened.

As they crossed the street, the first thing Chad saw was a police car with the light flashing. There were two officers talking to people in the park.

"Look!" Spike said. "What happened?"

"I think you're what happened, kid."

They approached one of the officers, who was talking to a woman and making notes on a pad. "Excuse me," Chad said. "You wouldn't be looking for a missing boy, would you?"

The policeman turned to Spike. "Are you Leon Rutledge?" he asked.

"Yeah, but everybody calls me Spike."

"I'm Dr. Chad Markham, from the clinic across the street." Taking out his wallet, Chad showed the officer his driver's license. "I'm also a neighbor of Spike's. He showed up in my office a little while ago with a bloody knee."

"Thank you for bringing him back, sir," the policeman said.

"He told me that he'd showed his injury to his Aunt Fiona and she told him to go away," Chad said. "Apparently he took her literally."

"She told you to go away?" the policeman asked Spike.

He nodded. "But I'm all right now. See?" He stretched his leg so the officer could see the bandage, which had pictures of Big Bird.

"Leon! Leon!" Aunt Fiona came running across the grass.

"Leon, you okay, my man?" Geoff loped alongside her.

Fiona glared at Chad. "I should have known he'd be with you. Jill's behind this, isn't she? What'd you do, sneak off with him just to make us look bad?"

"I was seeing patients until five minutes ago," Chad said quietly. To the policeman, he added, "You're welcome to check the records in pediatrics."

"That won't be necessary, sir," said the officer.

"Oh, so he's 'sir,' is he?" demanded Fiona. "You're ready to believe him and call me a liar, just like that!"

"Calm down," said her husband. "Nobody called you a liar. You didn't say you saw Chad take him, did you?"

"No," she admitted.

"We'll need to make a report on this," the officer said. "Are you the child's guardians?"

"We're going to be," Fiona answered.

"No, they aren't!" Spike said. "I live with Aunt Jill!"

"As you can see, there's a custody dispute," Chad explained. "The boy's parents died six months ago. He's lucky to have a lot of people who love him and want to take care of him."

To Fiona, the policeman said, "Do you have other children, ma'am?"

"No, of course not," she said. "Geoff and I got married last month."

"A word of advice. When a child comes to you for help, don't tell him to go away. As you can see, he took your words to heart."

Chad hoped the advice was having an impact, but Fiona didn't look chastened, only angry. It was Geoff who said, "We'll remember that, officer."

The policeman made another note and left. Chad offered to drive Spike home. Fiona and Geoff's motel was a block away, he pointed out, so there was no need for them to go.

"Tell Jill we'll be over at noon tomorrow to take him out again," Fiona said.

"Are you sure..."

"Today doesn't count. We need to get to know each other, that's all," she snapped.

As soon as she was gone, Spike said, "I don't want to go out with her tomorrow."

"I wish you didn't have to," Chad said. "But we can't afford to make an enemy of her."

"I wish the policemen would arrest her!"

"You know," he said, "we're going to have to walk right by that ice cream parlor to get to my car. I don't suppose you want a cone, do you?"

"Okay!" Spike smiled for the first time since he'd turned up.

WITHOUT A CHILD to look after, Jill had expected to get a lot done on Saturday. There was laundry, grocery shopping, weeding the front lawn, vacuuming, mopping, dusting and, above all, trying to figure out how to solve the Mrs. Claus problem before it ballooned out of proportion.

The mall staff had wrestled with the issue all week, even as remodeling proceeded on the Santa Around the World displays. They'd considered giving Mrs. Claus her own station, but, as luck would have it, there were only four tableaux in addition to the main, center court display. Sticking Marcia in an ordinary booth didn't show the right spirit.

But Jill couldn't concentrate on anything. She forgot her grocery list and had to improvise at the supermarket, with the result that she bought things she didn't need and forgot half of what she did.

She nearly caught Normal's tail in the vacuum because she didn't see him snoozing behind the couch. She mopped one bathroom floor twice by mistake.

She was worried about Spike. Not so much about the custody dispute, as about what was happening to him right now.

Was he too cold at the beach? Would Geoff and Fiona stay right next to him if he went into the water? He was too little to wade alone into the surf, where a riptide might catch him.

Jill was folding laundry when the truth hit her. Sometime during the past month she'd changed. She'd become a mother.

She had bonded so tightly with Spike that she drew his feelings right into her soul. The possibility of his being unhappy or frightened or in danger was ten times worse than if any of those things happened to her.

Jill nearly dropped the towel she was holding. She'd loved her nephew for a long time, but she'd never felt emotions this deep.

The anxiety was almost overpowering, until a reassuring image of Chad came to her, with his playful gray-green eyes and sun-streaked brown hair. He cared about Spike, too. If they needed him, she knew he would come through.

A few minutes later, when she saw the two of them walking toward the house together, it seemed like the most natural thing in the world.

"I WANT TO LET YOU KNOW how honored I am," Chad said as he cleared the table, "that you are entrusting me with the perilous and difficult task of cleaning up and loading the dishwasher."

He'd enjoyed Jill's cooking, even though she served far more fruits and vegetables than any normal man ate, and her rice was a suspicious brown color. The chicken had been tasty, considering that it wasn't deep-fried, and he'd actually liked the fat-free, no-sugar-added ice cream.

"Why is cleaning up perilous and difficult?" Spike asked. "And what's perilous mean?"

"It means dangerous. Dr. Chad is being funny," Jill told her nephew.

"I'm serious," he said. "You have no idea how often I break glasses and dishes. I could easily cut myself. Not to mention scattering shards of dangerous material on the floor and cutting my feet to shreds."

He glanced hopefully at Jill. Surely after this thinly veiled threat of calamity, she would want to scrape and load the dishes herself.

"I'll take my chances," she said. "You're not getting out of this, even if you are the hero of the day for rescuing Spike. Besides, you won't cut your feet because you're wearing shoes."

He reminded himself that she'd given him a hug this afternoon when he returned with Spike. And she'd smiled when he cleaned up the yard after his dogs. So he was in her good graces, but not enough to get out of doing the dishes. "Okay. I won't press the issue."

He kind of enjoyed the task, anyway, he decided a few minutes later as he worked. Jill had beautiful china dishes decorated with painted flowers and butterflies. Chad appreciated their feminine delicacy even though, unlike his plastic ones, they couldn't double as mock Frisbees.

And he enjoyed hearing the noises of a household around him: Spike laughing as he played in the other room with his teddy bears, Jill humming along with the radio while she reorganized her recipe box.

Chad tried to remember the sounds of his childhood. From his mother's home office had come the clack of her old typewriter and the occasional thump of a book being knocked over. His father, when he was home, had played classical music on the stereo. His collection was so old that the vinyl albums issued as many hisses and pops as mellow tones, but Chad had warm memories of Mozart and Chopin.

"What did your house sound like?" he asked.

"Excuse me?" Jill looked up from the recipe box.

"When you were growing up," he explained, wedging a pot into the dishwasher. "What kind of noises did people make? Did they listen to music? Watch the TV all the time?"

"My brother, Ellery, played the trumpet in the high school marching band," she said. "He used to practice in the garage, but we could still hear him. My mom's sewing machine whirred all the time, since she made most of our clothes. Dad watched game shows on TV."

"What was your father like?" Chad didn't recall hearing her mention him before.

"He was quite a bit older than Mom." Jill pointed toward the adjacent den, where photos filled a framed collage. "I've got a picture of them at their twentieth wedding anniversary. He sold life insurance."

"What did he die of?" Chad asked.

Her hand tightened on one of the cards. "Complications from diabetes."

He hadn't meant to open old wounds. To Chad, as a doctor, questions about people's medical problems came naturally, but now he wondered if he'd been insensitive.

"Sorry. It was none of my business." He poured detergent into the dishwasher, closed it and turned it on. "Isn't it Spike's bedtime?"

"Oh, right!" She put the recipes away.

The little boy didn't argue about going to bed. He scampered down the hall to change clothes, and in a few minutes was ready to read with Chad.

Jill and Spike were on the final chapter of *The Mouse and the Motorcycle*, he found when he opened to the bookmark. He made a mental note to go back and read the rest for himself.

As he read aloud, the boy picked out a couple of letters on the page and read the words *an* and *to*, although he pronounced it "toe."

"He learned that at preschool this week," Jill said.

"I'm impressed." Chad gave the boy a squeeze. "Smart kid."

"Aren't you going to say thank you?" Jill asked.

"Thank you." Spike's lip quivered. "Mom, you won't let Aunt Fiona take me away, will you?"

"I'll do everything in my power to prevent it," Jill said.

"Me, too," Chad promised.

"Okay." Spike buried his nose in his teddy bear.

They kissed the boy good-night and adjourned to the den. En route, Jill fixed them each a cup of green tea. Chad would normally have grabbed a soda, but she assured him that green tea was full of antioxidants and helped prevent heart attacks and cancer.

"How long have you been on this health kick?" he asked.

"My mom always encouraged us to eat well." Jill curled up on the couch beside him. "Then when I got pregnant..." She stopped abruptly.

A chill ran down Chad's spine. Jill didn't have a child of her own, so something had obviously gone wrong. "That must be a painful subject."

"Yes." A sweep of pale hair fell across her cheek as she ducked her head.

Okay, it was painful, but he hoped she'd say more. When she didn't, Chad knew better than to pry. "Eating a healthy diet must make you feel more in control of your life," he said, by way of returning to their earlier topic.

She pushed the hair back, and he saw that moisture had darkened her eyes to an almost midnight blue. "I got even more fanatical about it after my brother died. He worked long hours, and it made him impatient about balancing his insulin with his diet. Apparently he blacked out while driving."

"That was how he and his wife died?"

She nodded. "Now Spike depends on me, and even though I'm not diabetic, I refuse to take chances with my health."

Chad thought guiltily about doughnuts and pizza and fudge, and doubted he could give them up. He could live without beer and possibly coffee, and he wouldn't mind abandoning French fries, but fast-food hamburgers were another story. "I'm afraid I'm a failure in the healthy food department."

"I have to admit, the hardest part is eating whole-wheat pasta. It takes a while to get used to it." Jill tried to stifle a yawn. "Long day."

"Let's see what's on the news." Chad had no idea if it was time for a broadcast. He simply didn't want to part from her yet. "Put your head on my shoulder. You can nod off if you want."

"That wouldn't be polite." She nuzzled against him.

"Forget polite. I live here, remember?" He clicked on the TV. "Oh, wow, an old *Star Trek!* Does it look to you like Captain Kirk's wearing a girdle under that uniform?"

She chuckled and relaxed, her hair tickling his neck. Chad laid one arm around her. Just to steady her, of course.

As she breathed, he became aware of the rise and fall of her breast against his forearm. Surely she could feel it, too. He hoped the cheesy special effects on TV wouldn't have a dampening effect on her ardor. They certainly never affected him that way.

In fact, he was experiencing some special effects of his own, shimmering waves that raced through his bloodstream. Jill's silky blouse had fallen loose from her waistband, baring a strip of skin. When his wrist grazed it, the intimate contact sent Chad's imagination into high gear.

The fantasy: Jill seductively unbuttoned her shirt. The tops of her breasts swelled above a lacy brassiere, inviting his hands to cup them. Her chin tilted as she encouraged him to slide the straps down her arms. Their mouths met...

The reality: "I'd better go to bed. I'm falling asleep." Jill uncoiled from the sofa and stretched, seemingly unaware that her breasts were straining at the fabric. She murmured, "Sleep well," and retreated through the house.

Sleep? How could a man sleep when his body was on fire?

Grimly Chad tried to get comfortable on the couch. He wished those *Star Trek* guys would figure out that the monster killing people in a cave was merely protecting its young. You would think they'd remember it from having lived through that episode a zillion times. But no, it would take another Vulcan mind-meld for them to get the picture.

Something heavy plopped onto his lap. Chad gave a start, and received a plaintive ''meow'' in response.

He stared into the blue eyes of the black-and-white cat, Neurotic. He could have sworn it said, ''Quit wiggling and scratch me.''

With a groan Chad sank back to watch the rest of the episode and stroke the cat. He knew when he was licked.

JILL TOSSED IN BED, hearing the murmur of the TV from the den and wishing she hadn't mentioned her pregnancy to Chad.

It was amazing how he kept sneaking behind her defenses. This afternoon she'd been so glad to see him return with Spike that she'd thrown her arms around him.

Then tonight, on the couch, she couldn't believe she'd nearly fallen asleep in his arms. She supposed that to a guy it wasn't much of a compliment when a woman dozed off, but it indicated that she felt at home with him.

At home. But they were only pretending to live together. He wasn't her fiancé and he never would be, because she couldn't offer him what he wanted most.

Her inability to have children wasn't the only thing

keeping them apart, though. Much as Chad seemed to enjoy being with her and Spike, his humorous tone discouraged any deep emotional involvement. He was along for the good times, not the tough ones.

Right now they had two things in common: an attachment to Spike and a dislike of the Flora Dora Girls. Jill refused to fool herself into believing such a relationship could last.

Chapter Eleven

Ticket stub in hand, Chad surveyed the plush, vaulted lobby of the multiplex theater. He and Jill had both been so uncomfortable at entrusting the boy to his aunt and uncle that he'd decided to follow them. He'd come alone so he was less likely to be spotted.

According to the marquee, a Disney cartoon was the only G-rated movie playing on any of the theater's five screens. Fiona and Geoff must have already taken Spike inside.

He'd known where they were headed because they'd asked directions to the theater. Not wanting to be seen, he'd waited ten minutes and then driven over here. The sight of Geoff's Thunderbird in the parking garage had confirmed their presence.

He didn't suppose the child was likely to come to harm here. Even a scraped knee would be unusual in this setting. But Spike might wander out in search of the men's room by himself, something Jill would never allow. Chad didn't think a five-year-old should go to a public rest room alone, either, so he would keep his eyes open.

The animated feature, according to the ticket seller, was eighty-seven minutes long. He checked his watch and resolved to go outside with five minutes to spare, then linger across the street until he saw the three of them leaving.

A group of teenagers wandered across the lobby, munching candy bars and spilling popcorn. Chad wondered why fashion required them to wear clothes that were either tourniquet tight or as baggy as clowns. He supposed he was getting conservative at the advanced age of thirty-five.

He stretched, and watched a woman shepherd a couple of preteen girls toward an R-rated horror film on the far side of the lobby. Was she out of her mind? When he had kids, Chad vowed, he wouldn't even let them see a PG film without screening it first.

One of the girls reminded him of Eva, nurse Marie's younger daughter. When he'd first come to work at the inner-city hospital, Eva must have been about eleven, and had often dropped by after school to do her homework in the waiting room. He wondered how she and her brother and sister—and, especially, their mother—were faring in northern California.

Marie had moved last year, under circumstances that weren't entirely happy. Although Chad had sent his new work address when he changed jobs a few months later, he'd never heard from her.

A loud wail caught his attention, and he saw a small figure standing in the doorway of the horror-film theater. Spike!

Chad jumped to his feet, fury welling at the idiocy of taking the child to see an R-rated film. From the way the boy was sobbing, he'd been thoroughly frightened.

As Chad started forward, a knot of people surged in front of him, blocking his path. At the same time he saw a gray-haired couple stop to comfort Spike.

The inner door flew open, and Fiona burst out of the theater, followed by her husband. "Leon! You get back in here!"

Chad tried to angle around the people in front of him, but had to be patient a moment longer. From across the lobby, he heard the gray-haired man demand, "Is this your child?"

"Yes," Fiona snapped. "And I'll thank you to mind your own business."

"Wait a minute," Geoff said from behind her. "The kid's scared."

"He needs to stop being such a crybaby! You want to spend the rest of your life watching nothing but G-rated cartoons?" she demanded. "He'll get used to it."

"What a selfish attitude," the woman said. "I can't believe you're his mother."

"Well, I am!" Fiona said.

Spike glared at her. "You are not, and I'm not a crybaby, either. You're the one who cried in front of the policeman yesterday!"

That's telling her! Finally edging around the clump of people, Chad crossed the lobby.

"Daddy! Daddy!" Spike cried, spotting him, and pelted into Chad's arms.

"Hi, sport." He scooped up the little boy. "You did the right thing, leaving that scary movie. Sometimes kids have better sense than grown-ups."

Fiona stared daggers at him. "What're you doing here?"

"I figured I might take in a flick today, too," he said. The older couple, apparently satisfied by his intervention, moved on.

"Don't lie to me. You're spying," she said.

"Yeah. And a good thing he is," replied her husband. "Let's get out of here."

"But we already paid!"

"You said you don't want to see a cartoon, and he doesn't belong in an R-rated film," Geoff said. "Come on."

They exited into a narrow shopping street filled with eateries and curio stores. Noticing an ice cream parlor half a block away, Chad headed in that direction.

Fiona stumped alongside, her irritation unabated. "This is our time with Spike. We can do what we want."

"Oh, really?" Chad said. "When he has nightmares about that movie, are you going to sit up with him? Are you going to be the one to reassure him, at the expense of your own sleep? I don't think so."

"Those old people were right," Geoff said from behind them. "Fiona, you didn't sound like a mother to me, either."

"Well, I'm not! I'm an aunt! And so is Jill." She sniffed.

The ice cream store was busy, and Chad didn't relish having an audience for this quarrel. He was glad when Fiona piped down.

He ordered cones for himself and Spike and let the Wagners pay for their own ice cream. They adjourned outside to some empty tables and chairs.

Fiona refused to meet Chad's eye. Judging by the stubborn angle of her chin, she had no intention of conceding anything.

Geoff was halfway through his peppermint cone before he spoke again. "I think it's time we were honest," he told Chad. "This whole idea of adopting Leon was a spur-of-the-moment thing when the lawyer called and said he had a big inheritance.''

"What's that?'' Spike asked.

"Money,'' Chad said. "From your parents.''

"I've got as much right to it as anyone,'' Fiona said. "Leah was my sister.''

"The money isn't yours, it's your nephew's,'' Chad said. "From what I hear, it's going to be put into a trust, administered by some third party such as a bank.'' He deliberately made it sound as if the trust were a foregone conclusion.

"The money's for Leon's upkeep, isn't it?'' she challenged. "Whoever adopts him might need it to buy a new house or start a business, right? It would be for his own good.''

"You'd have to apply to the trustee,'' Chad said. "I doubt they'd agree. Except for out-of-pocket expenses such as food, clothing and medical care, it will probably be held for his education and turned over to him when he's an adult.''

Geoff started to whistle, but thanks to his chilled mouth only managed to blow out a bit of air. "There goes the repair shop we were discussing.''

"I don't believe it.'' Fiona didn't sound sure of herself, though. "It's Jill's doing, isn't it? And Ellery's mother, she's behind this. They don't want me to have him.''

"Come on, Fi, you're not ready to be stuck with a child,'' said her husband. "You can't even force yourself to sit through a G-rated movie.''

"Horror films never bothered me when I was a kid,'' she grumped.

"Every child is different,'' Chad said. "You have

to listen to them and find out who they really are and what they need.''

"I can figure it out as well as you can!"

Diplomacy clearly wasn't working. "Calling him a crybaby is like telling him to shut up," he said. "It cuts off communication."

"You're not even related to him—yet." Fiona plucked a cherry from her ice cream and popped it into her mouth. "You've got no right to tell anybody anything."

"Leon called him Dad," Geoff noted. "It seems to me the boy's already got a two-parent home."

Fiona chewed on her lower lip. Chad assumed she was searching for some way to hold on to what she had hoped would be a financial jackpot.

Finally she said, "We've got as good a case as they do. Just because they live in a fancier house, that shouldn't mean anything. But, Geoff, we have to both be in this together."

"Think about it," he said. "That trustee's not going to let us use the inheritance the way we want. What if we end up with the kid and no extra money?"

"I want him!" Fiona said. "I've got as much right as Jill does!"

Lowering his cone, Spike narrowed his eyes in a manner he must have seen on television. "I'll run away. I'll scream and kick you. I'll make you send me back to Aunt Jill."

"What a brat! Oh, all right," Fiona snarled at Chad. "You can keep him." Standing up, she yanked Geoff to his feet. "Let's go."

As her husband was hauled away, he called back, "Good luck, Leon. I like your attitude, dude."

Chad held up his hand for a high-five. Spike smacked it enthusiastically. "Does this mean we win?"

"That's exactly what it means," Chad said, beaming.

THAT NIGHT Jill did something she hardly ever even dreamed of doing. She sent out for pizza.

With it they drank champagne and, in Spike's case, grape juice. A candelabra that she hadn't used since her divorce blazed in the center of the table as a symbol of victory.

"Tell me again what that gray-haired lady said to Fiona," she begged Chad, and relished every detail as he patiently retold the tale.

"Don't forget Spike's part," he noted over his third slice of supreme. "He stood tough."

"He had every right to!" she said. "It's his life, and his inheritance, too."

"You can have my money, Aunt Jill," Spike told her. "I wouldn't mind giving it to you."

"I don't want your money. I want you." The champagne made her cheeks hot, or maybe that was pure happiness. "Chad, I don't know how to thank you. If you hadn't posed as my fiancé, they wouldn't have backed down."

"You're not really getting married?" Spike asked.

Embarrassed, Jill glanced at Chad. The one part of this business that she regretted was the need to practice a deception, particularly in front of the child. "We...haven't exactly..."

"Not right away," Chad said. "It's something for us to consider in the future, though."

Jill got a quivery sensation in her stomach. Did he mean that? She wished there were some easy way to break the truth to him. *Chad, I can't have children of my own. Feel free to...*

To what? Abandon her? Act like a jerk?

She couldn't say those things, and she decided it wasn't the right time to broach the subject, anyway. She didn't want to put a space between them. Not tonight, when he'd saved Spike, and her, from years of misery.

When they put Spike to bed, he fell asleep within minutes. She hoped his triumph over Fiona had canceled his scary experience at the horror movie.

"I realized something yesterday," Jill admitted as she and Chad left the room. "With Spike, I feel the same pain or fear or anxiety I imagine he must be feeling. It's as if he were an extension of myself."

In the faint light he studied her. "That's because you have a great capacity for love."

"Everyone has that, unless there's something seriously wrong with them," she said.

He shook his head. "Not if they're self-absorbed, like Fiona. Of all the people I've met, and I meet quite a few in my line of work, you're one of the most open and tenderhearted."

"Are those synonyms for being a sucker?" She meant to tease, but the words came out more serious than intended. "I mean, after my divorce, I didn't feel very loving. Or very lovable."

They went down the hall into the den. Chad knelt by the stereo system and found a mellow station on the radio. "That ex-husband of yours sounds like a Grade-A loser. He really did a number on your self-confidence."

He came to sit beside Jill on the couch. When he sank down, his weight made the cushions dip, and she slid against him. She didn't try to move away, because she didn't want to.

"He had an affair with his assistant at work," she admitted. "I think it was his cowardly way of breaking off the marriage without having to be honest about his feelings. Besides, she was fresh out of college and practically worshipped him."

"The way you probably did, when you first met him," he guessed.

The comment surprised Jill. "I suppose I did." She'd been twenty-five, just getting established in her career and a bit overwhelmed by Gary, who was a successful businessman at thirty-one. "He was a little older and impressive in a lot of ways. But during four years of marriage, I grew up."

"Maybe he had a hard time dealing with a woman as an equal," he said.

"I wish he'd simply said he didn't want to be stuck with me anymore." Chad was such a good listener that the words poured out. "Instead I had to find out one clue at a time, and after the truth became obvious, I realized everyone else in his office already knew what was going on. It was ugly and cheap and worst of all..." She had to stop, because tears welled close to the surface.

"If you tell me the rest," he said, "I'll promise to fetch the tissues."

Despite herself, Jill smiled. "I won't need them. I'm done crying over that loser. Here goes, then. The worst part was that having my husband sleep with another woman was like announcing to the world that there was something missing, something I couldn't give him."

And there had been, of course. Something that, even now, she couldn't bear to bring up.

Chad cupped her chin in his palm and studied her as if he were planning to paint a portrait. "I don't see anything missing."

"I didn't mean it literally." Her pulse beat faster.

"It seems to me that, in my capacity as rescuer of the day, I have one more duty to perform." Before she could reply, Chad's lips closed over hers. The contact sent a silvery weakness flooding all the way to her wrists and knees. When he lifted his head, he said, "Nope, nothing missing."

Jill knew she was treading on thin ice, but she couldn't resist. "You can't tell from one little kiss."

"Is that a challenge?"

She ought to leave well enough alone. In fact, she ought to flee the room. Instead she said, "It isn't a challenge, it's an observation."

"You're right. And as a scientist I believe in conducting thorough research." Taking her into the circle of his arms, Chad explored her mouth slowly and deliberately.

Champagne fizzed in her bloodstream. Jill slipped her arms around his neck and kissed him harder.

Dreamily she registered the pressure of his hand on her lower back, holding her tight, as his tongue grazed the inside of her cheek. Her body prickled with excitement. The stretch velour of her top molded itself to her breasts, and her skirt hiked tantalizingly along her thighs. When his fingers stroked her leg, she found she didn't want him to stop.

He was completely different from her husband, the only man she'd ever made love with. Chad took his time, letting the anticipation build. He gazed at her as though he truly enjoyed seeing her reaction.

With Gary, despite his practiced skill, there'd always

been something rushed about their lovemaking. Jill suspected he'd only pretended that he cared about her response. His own pleasure was the sole thing that mattered to him.

With Chad, she found, there was importance in each movement, each caress. She wanted him to claim each part of her, to banish the old painful memories and replace them with new ones.

When he unbuttoned her blouse, the whisper of his breath across her bare skin thrilled her almost beyond bearing. She helped him lower her bra, and, when he caught the peaks between his lips, white-hot fire shot into her core.

Chad looked up. "We should go somewhere more private." His voice had a raw, husky quality.

Moving into the bedroom would mean committing herself to a course she wasn't sure she was ready to follow. Sitting up, Jill straightened her clothing and tried to think clearly.

She ought to say good-night and go to bed alone. Chad would be leaving next weekend for a nine-day skiing trip with his buddies. Even after he returned, he wasn't a man she could count on to stick around.

Yet, tonight, she wanted to wipe away the soul-deep pain that Gary's rejection had inflicted. She wanted to know another man, a good man, and to experience her own body as an implement of soaring passion. Just this once.

"Yes," she said. "Let's go." And held out her hand.

CHAD HADN'T EXPECTED Jill to agree. Even when his instincts told him that she was as ready as he was to move to the next step, he'd been prepared for her to slam the door in his face.

Now, half-dazed, he went down the hall with her to the master bedroom. He hadn't even entered the room before, and yet he knew it at once. The floral scent, the sensuous curves of the modern furniture and the mellow glow of the bedside lamp suited her exactly.

Inside, Jill glanced at him with a sweet uncertainty that stirred his heart. Her hands fluttered as if unsure which item to remove first, and then she sat on the edge of the bed and slipped off her shoes.

Chad eased himself down beside her, watching the play of light across her delicate features. With that wealth of silver-blond hair and those wide, blue eyes, she was like a fantasy woman, and yet he knew how real she was.

"From some angles, a man could say you were beautiful," he teased as he helped her roll off her pantyhose.

"Oh?" Her inquisitive gaze met his. "Which angles?"

Holding her legs across his lap and peeling away the nylon, he said, "This one, for example." Her legs were smooth and slim, inviting long strokes. "Also—" he opened her blouse and slid down her bra straps "—definitely this one."

With a taunting smile she swung her legs off his lap and turned her back on him. "How do I look from this perspective?"

He lifted the rich mane of hair and kissed her neck. "Beautiful. I guess you don't have any bad angles."

Twisting her hair in his hand, he guided her around until their gazes met. Then he kissed her again while he lowered her across the bed.

Poised over her, he removed her bra, along with the blouse. Her breasts were small and firm, wonderfully round below the vulnerable pulse of her throat.

He cupped them in his hands, and his whole body hardened. He fought to restrain the impulse to take her quickly. There was something ethereal, almost fragile, about Jill.

As he hesitated, she loosened his shirt, and he shrugged it off. To his gratification she was already removing his belt, and soon the rest of his clothes hit the floor as well.

They lay with lamplight flowing across their bare skin, highlighting their wonderful mounds and tantalizing recesses. "Did I say you were beautiful?" Chad sighed. "Make that, absolutely glorious."

He raised himself over her. Jill's hand touched his shoulder, almost in supplication, and then she closed her knees and moved a little away from him in sudden shyness.

Chad spread her hair across the pillow. He leaned over her, his body nuzzling hers in the most erotic places, while his tongue traced her temple and the curve of her ear. Beneath him, her knees parted.

She caught his mouth with hers and moved lightly against him. He kissed her and, at the same time, inserted himself gently but firmly between her legs.

A small cry escaped her, and she gripped his shoulders. Although Chad knew he should go slowly, the pleasure spreading through him took on a life of its own, and he thrust into her with a sense of coming home.

He gazed down at where their hips joined. Her hair was silvery there, too, and her slender thighs surrounded him in feminine invitation.

He withdrew and then took her again with growing intensity. Her back arched, and her breasts rose toward him until he bent and claimed the nipples. Crying out, Jill caught his hips.

She was more than Chad had imagined possible, more a part of him, more attuned to his rhythms and his needs. He'd never known a woman so fierce and so dainty at the same time.

He wasn't sure how long he could hold himself in check. Not much longer. Minutes. Seconds. Now!

SO THIS WAS WHAT all the fuss was about, Jill thought wildly—this glorious sense of physical abandon. She'd never experienced anything like it with Gary.

Her breasts pressed into Chad's chest and her legs tangled with his. There were so many starry points of contact, each more marvelous than the last. If only she could touch him everywhere at once.

A fine sheen covered his body as Chad bucked hard inside her, demanding, merging, fusing the two of them into one white-hot being. Jill writhed against him. She felt herself incandescing, losing awareness of anything except this sensual explosion.

At last the flames died to a residual radiance. Much as she hated to leave that moment of pure ecstasy, Jill savored the precious gift she had received.

It was the gift of her own sensuality. Now she knew that not only hadn't Gary destroyed it, he'd never truly inspired it in the first place.

Chapter Twelve

As he lay beside Jill, Chad mused that things hadn't turned out the way he'd expected.

After a lifetime of working too hard and caring too much, he'd switched a year ago to a less stressful job and resolved to indulge himself. Under most circumstances, sex certainly fell into the category of self-indulgence, but what he'd just experienced was something else entirely.

At the height of his exhilaration, he hadn't been just a guy enjoying physical release. He'd become part of something bigger, as if their physical union had forged a profound emotional connection between him and Jill.

What was going on here? They'd only known each other for a few weeks. It was too soon to read anything into it, and yet their lovemaking had changed him in a way he didn't understand.

He felt a great warmth toward her, but what did it mean? He must be careful not to blurt out some foolish declaration of love. Love was a distant territory that he couldn't have reached yet, because he hadn't made a long enough journey.

Rolling toward her, Chad smiled at the sight of the fine-boned woman curled with a sheet draped across her waist. Golden skin, silvery hair, soft breasts. Oh, heavens, he was stirring again.

He sat up and finger combed back his hair. "Wow."

"I guess that expresses my sentiments, too." Jill's face shone.

He enjoyed the way her gaze caressed his bare chest, and wondered if she could see how, beneath the sheet, he'd grown hard. "This calls for a rematch."

"I don't think..." She stopped, as if becoming aware of something. He learned what it was a moment later, when she said, "We didn't use any protection."

It hadn't even occurred to him. As a doctor, it should have. Chad supposed this was the result of his having led too chaste a life for too long, but that was no excuse. "I'm sorry."

She drew her knees to her chest and hugged them. "I don't suppose anything's likely to happen."

"If it does, you know how I feel about kids." He reached for her and was startled to see her flinch. "Did I say something wrong?"

She rested her cheek atop her knees, letting her hair spill like a cloud over her legs. "No. It's just that I should have shown better judgment."

"You're not telling me you regret making love?" He would sooner believe that the Wright Brothers had regretted learning how to fly.

"No." She'd withdrawn from him, though, behind a screen of lowered eyelashes. "I think, in a way, it was good for both of us. But now we have to go back to the way we were before."

"And what way is that?" he demanded.

"Friends. Neighbors." She stared down at her feet as if she found them fascinating.

"You're kidding!" He battled the impulse to catch her chin and force her to meet his eyes.

"We don't even really know each other," Jill said.

"We know each other a lot better than we did an hour ago," Chad said.

A reluctant smile tugged her lips. "That's true."

"What's come over you?" As soon as he asked the question, the answer hit him. "I guess this is what they call postcoital panic."

"Excuse me?" she asked. "Is that a medical term?"

"Informally." Chad ached to draw her close, but he didn't want to risk making her flinch again. "You need space. In a few days you'll see that this could be the beginning of—"

He stopped. A few minutes ago he'd warned himself not to jump to conclusions. Especially not aloud.

"The beginning of what?" Jill asked.

"A very good time," he said. "A lot of fun. You have to admit, what happened tonight gives new meaning to the phrase *pleasure principle*."

"I concede the point," she said. "But I stand by my position. Fun isn't enough for me."

He hadn't meant *fun* in the shallow sense that she implied. Or had he? Chad wondered.

He hated being so confused, but he couldn't think straight while his manly portion was playing havoc with the smooth line of the sheet. Some solitude and a chance to focus his thoughts on, say, L.A.'s prospects of landing another pro football team, ought to take care of the problem.

Then he'd be free to think about Jill and what she meant to him and what he wanted to mean to her. And how much he yearned to whip that sheet off her naked body.

This wasn't helping his physical situation. "What do you want me to do?"

"I think it would be best if you went to your own room."

"You're kidding!"

"You aren't angry, are you?"

"Nothing I can't handle." He made a twirling gesture with his forefinger. "Turn around, okay? If you're not going to ravish my body, I'd prefer a little privacy."

Jill swung away, and he found himself staring at a cascade of moonlit hair and a slim back that curved into a deliciously rounded bottom.

From all angles he reflected ruefully, she was indisputably beautiful. And from all angles he was indisputably aroused by her.

THE DOOR CLOSED QUIETLY behind Chad. *So what were you hoping for, a declaration of undying devotion?* Jill demanded of herself.

She huddled on her side of the bed, reluctant to stretch into the residual warmth left where he had been lying moments before. She'd made the choice to go to bed with him when they'd only known each other a short time, so why be displeased that he considered it merely fun?

Relationships took time to grow. Besides, she'd known in advance that this one faced an insurmountable obstacle.

Restlessly Jill went to shower in her private bathroom. Maybe she was so edgy because of the danger of a pregnancy that could threaten her life, she reflected, as the hot water sluiced over her steamy skin.

Her obstetrician had recommended surgery to end

the possibility of ever running that risk again. But since she and Gary split up, Jill hadn't been involved with anyone else. She'd accepted the idea that she probably never would find a man she could trust, so there'd seemed no point in going through the expense and trauma of sterilization.

Besides, the word distressed her. Sterile. She knew that being unable to have children didn't make her empty and bleak the way the term implied. She was full of warmth and life, sexually responsive—as she'd proven to herself tonight—and capable of giving Spike all the maternal nurturing he needed. Still, words had power, and she hadn't been ready to accept the devastation of that one.

Jill stepped from the shower and toweled off. She began to smile at her own foolishness. Hardly anyone got pregnant from having sex just once, so what was she worried about?

Ellery and Leah had tried for a year before Spike was conceived. Her longtime best friend, Kathryn, who now lived in Denver, had undergone extensive fertility treatments before giving birth to twins. The chances of Jill's being pregnant were practically zero.

And she wasn't going to sleep with Chad again. So what could it hurt if she let her mind replay the powerful way he'd held himself over her, his arm muscles bulging, his chest gleaming in the lamplight.

The sensation when he'd entered her had been transcendent. She might as well enjoy the memory, since she would never again experience the reality.

Jill folded the towel onto the rack. The real challenge would be trying to get some sleep.

She ought to be glad Chad was going home tomorrow. At least her life could return to normal.

SHE COULDN'T RESIST driving by his house Monday on the way to work. Chad had left before breakfast, saying only a polite farewell and shepherding his dogs through the back fence.

Jill told herself she wanted to see whether his house now conformed to the association's code. It wouldn't hurt if she caught a glimpse of him, either.

I don't want it to be over. Do I really have to accept that it is?

The painters still needed to finish the trim on the outside, she saw. But, through the curtainless windows, the electric-yellow interior nearly blinded her.

"Cool!" crowed Spike. "Can we paint our living room like that, Aunt Jill?"

She chuckled. "I don't have an electric-yellow personality like Chad does."

"Is he going to tuck me into bed tonight?" her nephew asked. "He could stay with us all the time. That would be nice."

"He has his own home." To change the subject she said, "Christmas is three weeks away. Do you know what you want?"

"That's up to Santa Claus," he said. "He always figures it out."

Until now Jill hadn't given much thought to the intricacies of Christmas gift giving. Leah must have bought the presents on the sly, wrapped and hidden them. And she'd obviously known exactly what suited her son.

Shopping for gifts wouldn't be difficult, since Jill worked at a mall. However, she had only the vaguest idea of what Spike might like, and she would hate to disappoint him.

Inspiration struck. "I'll bet you used to write to Santa, didn't you?"

"Oh, yeah, that's right," he said.

"Did you dictate the list to your mother? I mean, tell it to her?"

"That's right." His eyes widened. "Will you write it down for me, Aunt Jill?"

"You bet!" She didn't suggest that he talk to the Santa at the mall. She would have to take the boy around to all five of them or be accused of favoritism. Besides, she needed that list for herself.

"Can we do it tonight?" he asked.

"Sure." Jill couldn't wait to get started on her shopping. Besides, it would give them both something to keep their minds off the empty guest room.

After delivering Spike to the learning center, Jill parked her car and set out to walk the mall. The holiday magazines had arrived, so she replaced the older throwaways in the racks with the new publications.

Most of the stores had put up holiday decorations by last Friday, but Bertha Covens, the owner of Baby and Bath, waved to her from the display window. She was, Jill saw, arraying Christmas- Hanukkah- and Kwanza-themed towels and layette sets.

"I should have done this last weekend," the dark-haired woman explained as she emerged, dusting her hands on a teddy-bear-embroidered apron. "My son was supposed to help me take down the Mother Goose display and install my winter wonderland, but the surf was up. I should have spanked that boy more when I had the chance."

Jill gave a sympathetic nod. "Is he coming by today?"

"Yes, but my van's in the shop. I don't know how I'm going to cart off the old display."

The Mother Goose exhibit occupied a back corner of the store. As Jill recalled it included a cute little house open at one side, with cutout board figures from fairy tales spilling into the open.

"What are you planning to do with it?" she asked.

"Donate it to a children's home," Bertha said.

"Do you suppose I could borrow it?" Jill asked. "We might need to do a little redecorating to make it into a house for Mrs. Claus, but I doubt the children's home would mind."

"I'll tell you what," the shopkeeper said. "If you'll take responsibility for delivering it when you're done, you can have it."

"Perfect." Jill shook hands with her. "I'll send a crew down this morning."

As she headed for her office, her mind played over the mall's layout. There was a corner on the upper floor where the merchants had been complaining they weren't drawing enough customers.

There should be room for Mrs. Claus's house. The mall could provide cookies for Marcia to give away. That should draw lots of people and make Marcia happy, too.

Jill found herself humming happily. The day was off to a good start, after all.

ON FRIDAY, his first night at the A-frame cabin in Colorado, Chad left the pullout bed to an overweight, snoring friend of Vic's and slept in the narrow attic. He nearly suffocated. Cara and Shelly had insisted the heater be cranked up, and the hot air rose until it nearly gave him heat stroke.

He hadn't been sleeping well all week, anyway. He missed Jill and he'd had to do battle daily with the urge to drop by her house. But he intended to respect her feelings, at least until he sorted out his own.

The second night in Colorado, Chad's legs hurt too much from skiing for him to climb two flights of steps, so he pitched his sleeping bag in the dining room. Unfortunately it blocked the only route to the kitchen, and, in the dark, some would-be-refrigerator-raider tripped over him.

A slippered foot dug into his ribs, and he heard a muffled "Oof!" It sounded feminine, but before he regained the ability to breathe without blinding pain, she vanished. He didn't hear so much as a hint of an apology.

The next morning Vic finished a long call on his cell phone and came to Chad with a grim expression. "I'm afraid I've got some bad news."

His gut twisted. Was it about Jill or Spike? Then he remembered that there was no reason for anyone to call Vic about them.

"Yes?" Chad asked, more grumpily than he'd intended. His ribs still ached from last night.

"That was my dad," Vic said. "He really misses Torero and Blitz. I, uh, promised I'd get them back."

Chad glowered at him. He wasn't actually displeased. Although he'd liked the idea of taking the dogs, he hadn't expected to find them so undisciplined.

On the other hand he'd grown somewhat attached to them. "I don't know," he said. "We've kind of bonded."

"I'll repay what you've spent on their upkeep," Vic offered. "Including the kennel while you're on this trip."

Under other circumstances it might have been an attractive offer, but Chad was in no mood to let his friend off easily. "Jill and Spike are really fond of them, too." As long as he was stooping to wild exaggerations, he added, "In fact, I promised the boy we'd hook them up to a sled for Christmas and pretend we were in Alaska."

It was the most preposterous story he could think of, but Vic bought it. "Gee, man, I'm really sorry."

From the kitchen Cara emerged with a cup of hot chocolate. She made her way rather unsteadily toward the dining room table.

"What's wrong with her?" Chad asked. "Too much skiing?"

"I guess so," Vic said. "She hurt her foot."

A suspicion hit Chad. "Which part of it?"

"What do you mean, which part?"

"Heel or toe?" he said.

Cara winced as she pulled out a chair and, bending down, rubbed her toe. She didn't acknowledge the two men.

Chad knew guilt when he saw it. That stubbed toe had come at his expense, and the coward still wasn't apologizing.

"I'll let you have the dogs on one condition," he told Vic.

"Sure. Anything!"

"I sleep in your bedroom. Alone. For the rest of the week," Chad said.

"Whoa!" His friend regarded him in dismay. "There're two of us in there, you know."

"Cara's always cold. She'll love the attic," he said. "It reaches at least 120 degrees Fahrenheit up there."

The man glanced anxiously toward his girlfriend. "I don't think she'll go for it."

"Or you can pitch your blankets in the dining room." Chad raised his voice a little. "It'll make it easier for her to raid the refrigerator in the middle of the night."

The back of Cara's neck, which was all he could see of her skin, flushed crimson.

"Is there something I don't know?" Vic asked.

Cara faced them, her cheeks blazing. "He can have the room."

When his friend hesitated, Chad said, "Take it or leave it."

"Done." Vic shook hands on the deal. "My dad will be glad to get the dogs back."

"I'm going to miss them." Mostly Chad would miss the way the two animals howled and threw themselves at the side yard fence whenever the Flora Dora Girls walked by with their miniature poodle. It always made the sisters walk faster.

It was pure luxury to move into the bedroom after two days as a gypsy, he reflected a short time later. But his victory rang hollow.

He wished he had someone to share it with. And he wondered what that someone was doing now and whether she missed him.

ON SUNDAY, a week after Jill had made love with Chad, her mother brought over a Christmas tree she'd bought at a charity fund-raiser. About five feet high with full, bright-green branches, it filled the living room with the scent of pine.

"I knew it would be perfect," Nita announced as

she held the trunk steady. "I wanted to be sure my grandson got a tree this year."

Kneeling, Jill adjusted the screws in the tree stand. Around her, needles showered onto a fluffy, white circular cloth that protected the carpet.

"Can we hang candy canes?" Spike bounced excitedly around them. "Let's make popcorn and string it! Mom and I did that last year."

"How about if we make the popcorn and eat it instead?" Jill replied. "Look at the toy soldiers I bought for ornaments. And the little drums and bugles. I thought you'd like them."

"They're cute." Spike began taking the ornament soldiers out of their box.

"So when will Chad get home from Colorado?" Nita asked. "We should invite him to join us for Christmas dinner."

Jill struggled not to reveal the sudden tension in her throat. "He'll be back a week from today. And I don't think that's a good idea."

"Why not?" asked her mother.

Because I miss him too much already, and I don't want to get any closer. If I do, sooner or later I'm going to have to tell him the truth and watch that shuttered expression come over his face as he withdraws.

"It's too personal," Jill said. "Our first Christmas without Ellery and Leah."

"All the more reason to have a distraction," her mother said. "But I'll leave it up to you. Feel free to bring him along that evening—4 p.m. at my house."

Spike looked up from where he was parading the soldiers along the coffee table. "Please invite Chad. I want to see him!"

"Don't forget, his birthday is two days before

Christmas,'' Jill said. "Wouldn't you rather help him celebrate that? He said he never got a party when he was a little boy, so maybe we can take him some presents and balloons and cake.''

"And ice cream,'' Spike said.

As soon as he said those magic words, Jill knew he'd accepted the substitute celebration. "Okay.''

While she didn't relish throwing the man a mini-birthday party, it would be less emotional than sharing Christmas. With luck she could find some excuse to leave after an hour.

She might have diverted the boy's attention but not her mother's. When Spike wandered off to play in the den, she said, "Is there anything you want to tell me about Chad?''

Jill regarded the tree. It was as straight as she could make it. "He painted his living room electric-yellow.''

"Why is this a problem?'' her mother asked.

"It isn't.'' She drew a deep breath. "Except that in some ways he doesn't seem entirely grown-up.''

"Which ways?'' Nita probed. "Aside from his atrocious taste in decorating.''

"I don't think he's ready for the responsibility—no, that's not fair.'' Jill brushed the bangs off her forehead. "He'd be perfect for some woman, but, Mom, you know what I've been through. A man would have to accept a heck of a lot to marry me.''

"And you don't think Chad can handle it?'' she asked. "Maybe you underestimate him.''

"And maybe I'm not foolish enough to kid myself,'' Jill said tartly. "What he wants out of a relationship is fun and games.''

"Did he tell you so?'' Nita drew a strand of multicolored lights from a box and wove it through the tree branches.

"Yes."

That ended the argument. Jill should have been pleased, but she wasn't.

It was only later, when she was alone reading through Spike's list for Santa and figuring how much everything would cost, that she realized why she felt so disappointed.

She'd been hoping Nita could argue her into believing that she and Chad had a chance together. In defeating her mother's defense of him, Jill had defeated her own hopes, too.

Chapter Thirteen

By the middle of the week, Chad's body ached from skiing, and his cheeks smarted every time he poked his head into the chill air. He supposed that Coloradans considered southern Californians to be lightweights. Well, they were right.

At least he was sleeping decently, although Cara and Vic seemed grumpier than usual, he mused as he strolled down the main street of the resort town. He'd chosen to skip the slopes today and shop for presents.

Wreaths and bells glittered from lampposts, and colored lights blinked along the eaves of the shops. Chad wondered what sort of decorations coordinated with an electric-yellow living room, and decided there weren't any. Well, he didn't have anyone to decorate for, anyway.

He would have to give Jill and Spike their presents on Christmas Eve, since he was working at the clinic on the holiday. It had seemed reasonable for him to sign up for a shift, since he didn't have a family.

Someday he would, Chad mused as he stared in the window of a toy shop. Someday he'd have a wife and kids to gather around the tree.

There'd be a little girl who would love that brightly

clad African-American doll—which was perfect for Alicia, he thought, remembering Cynthia's daughter. And he'd have a son who'd get a kick out of helping him assemble that model airplane. Someone just like Spike.

Chad went inside and made the purchases, along with a couple of smaller souvenir gifts for Spike. A few doors farther along, he stopped at a bookstore and found a nonfiction book that Cynthia had mentioned wanting to read, and a Miss Manners book for Cara. He added the latest Tom Clancy thriller for Vic.

Now what was he going to get for Jill? What could be special enough, but not too intimate? Lingerie was probably out, he conceded as he passed another shop window. Especially that scarlet satin set with black lace trim.

He'd love to see it on her, though. Maybe she'd be willing to model it, as her Christmas present to him. On second thought, maybe not.

A health food store caught his attention. Chad recalled seeing another store from the same chain in Flora Vista. He supposed he could buy a gift certificate, but that didn't seem very romantic.

Down the block, the glass door of a beauty parlor swung open with a shiver of tiny bells. He halted in midstride, staring at the froth of silver-blond hair emerging into the crisp mountain air. What was Jill doing here?

Holding the door open with her shoulder, the woman tightened her coat belt, face averted. When she stepped clear, Chad saw with a plunge of dismay that her nose was too wide and her eyes too dark. It wasn't Jill.

A longing gripped him, so fierce that his lungs hurt.

What was he doing here, miles away, wasting his time, when he could be with the woman he…loved?

The air squeezed out of his lungs. Chad stood rock still, scarcely noticing the other shoppers edging past him. The silver-blonde, after shooting him a puzzled look, vanished in the throng.

She was the wrong woman. Every woman in the world was the wrong woman, except Jill.

He tried to examine this idea rationally. At the same time he forced his feet to start moving, because otherwise they were likely to end up frostbitten, not to mention trampled.

He'd believed that when he fell in love, he would know it immediately. Instead it had sneaked up on him.

Maybe if he'd declared himself to Jill while they were lying in bed together, she wouldn't have been so eager to return to a platonic relationship. Or perhaps while he'd been away she'd discovered that she missed him as much as he missed her.

Chad didn't relish looking like a fool, but he didn't fear taking risks, either. And this sounded like the kind of risk worth running.

Why should he and Jill spend the next months waving over the backyard fence and using Spike as an excuse to get together on rare occasions? The New Year was coming up and, with it, a time for new beginnings.

He began to whistle as he realized what it was that he wanted to buy her. It seemed a good omen when, on his way, he passed an antiques shop and spotted a weather vane topped by a very ugly green leprechaun.

It would annoy the dickens out of the Flora Dora Girls. This day was turning out to be more productive than he had expected.

THE CHRISTMAS SHOPPING season was in full swing. At the concierge desk, Jill helped Rose Rodgers tally the gift certificates for the Frequent Shoppers.

"People keep stopping by and saying how much they love the new international Santas!" Rose told her.

"That's funny, considering how much they hated them before." As soon as the words were out of her mouth, Jill wondered where that negative attitude had come from. She'd become grumpy the past few days and hoped it wasn't from anxiety about Chad's return.

She knew he must have arrived by nine last night, because she'd heard the dogs barking. He hadn't called, though. She supposed he'd been tired and had a lot of unpacking to do, but she'd hoped he would at least let her know he was safe.

He hadn't called from Colorado all week, either. Of course, she was the one who'd said she wanted to go back to being just friends. And she'd meant it.

Part of her had, anyway. The part that did the thinking and not the feeling.

"Jill?" Rose asked. "You've been daydreaming a lot lately. Are you all right?"

"Just preoccupied." With a rueful smile she stood up. "I haven't finished shopping for Spike. I'll do it on my lunch hour."

"You look a little flushed," Rose said. "I hope you aren't getting sick."

"I don't feel sick," she assured the marketplace manager. But a few minutes later, after breaking her dietary code and sampling one of Mrs. Claus's cookies, Jill suffered a queasy sensation.

She hoped there was nothing wrong with the treats. No one else seemed affected by them, though.

"It's wonderful having my own booth!" Marcia

gushed from the courtyard of the made-over Mother Goose house. "Can we do this every year?"

"We'll probably build even better displays, after the publicity we're receiving." The story of the international Santas had been covered in the local paper and picked up by a national wire service. Customers were visiting from far beyond the mall's primary and secondary market areas, ten to twenty miles away, and even its tertiary area, up to thirty miles away. One couple had come all the way from Arizona.

"Thanks," Marcia said. "If it weren't for you, this whole situation would have been a big mess."

That made Jill feel better. Her upset stomach lasted until lunchtime when, again fudging on her regime, she indulged in a baked potato with cheese. If she weren't careful, she'd grow round enough to pose as Santa Claus herself.

When she picked up Spike, his friend Matt Billings's mother, Sharon, asked if he could spend the night at their house. "It's Matt's birthday," she explained. "I told him he could invite a friend to sleep over. I can take them directly to school tomorrow."

Jill had no experience with child sleepovers, but Sharon seemed to consider the matter routine. "Spike, would you like to stay at Matt's house tonight?"

"Yes!" He jumped in the air. "Please, please, please!"

"I'll follow you home," Sharon said. "He won't need to pack much, just pajamas, a change of clothes, his toothbrush and that all-important stuffed animal."

At home Spike was ready in ten minutes. Jill, who'd bought a box of candy as part of Yvette's Christmas present, gave it to Matt for his birthday. She could always buy another one tomorrow.

"My favorite!" he cried. "Look, Mom, nuts!"

"I can tell you're an experienced mother," Sharon said. "Keeping a few spare gifts on hand is a real life-saver, isn't it?"

"Sure is." Jill decided not to admit it was pure luck.

After waving farewell, she went into the house alone. How strange it felt, not to have Spike around, she thought as she fed the cats.

He was too young for her to experience empty-nest syndrome, but already she got an inkling of what it must be like as children grew older and went their own ways. Of course, it would be easier if she had a younger child, someone with whom to experience the precious moments for a second time.

Jill's vision clouded with tears.

No matter how hard she tried to reconcile herself to the inevitable, she wanted more children. Rationally, she knew she could adopt, but her gut-level yearning refused to listen to reason.

The doorbell rang. Spike must have forgotten something, Jill thought. She wiped her eyes on a tissue and went to answer it.

There was no one on the porch, just a spectacularly ugly leprechaun weather vane propped against a post. Taped to its chest, a hand-lettered sign read: "Go to Chad's house. Take me with you."

That man was hopeless! Trust him not to announce his return with a simple phone call, but with a prank that made her smile through her tears.

Jill went out the back door, carrying the weather vane. She didn't want to walk down the street with it. If the Flora Dora Girls saw her, they'd consider her a partner in whatever crime Chad intended to commit, most likely stationing it on his roof.

When she let herself through the gate, she noticed that the dogs weren't around. She didn't hear them howling in the garage, either.

Her tap on the rear sliding-glass door stirred quick-moving footsteps within the house. The interior was semidark, and she didn't see Chad until he appeared at the door.

When he opened it, she caught a whiff of pine scent and a trace of antiseptic. The mountain sun had streaked his brown hair with even more gold than usual, and his bangs had grown long enough to flop over his forehead. She wanted to touch that hair and press her nose to his cheek to inhale his scent.

They stared at each other without speaking, and then he gripped her by the waist and pulled her against him. He tasted even better than he looked, his mouth urgent, his heat banishing the emptiness. Almost before Jill knew it, he'd closed the door, dropped the leprechaun on the floor and whisked her into the shadowed recesses of the house.

During a rare moment between kisses, he muttered, "Where's Spike?"

"Friend's house," she managed. "Overnight."

"Perfect." He scooped her into his arms.

Too surprised to protest, Jill held tight to his shoulders and let Chad carry her through the kitchen and down the hall. She hadn't meant to do this. Not to get close to him, certainly not to join him in the privacy of his bedroom.

It was a perfectly respectable man's room, with dark woods and no hint of electric-yellow, she noticed, as he swung her onto the bed. Yet there was nothing respectable about the way he set about stripping off her clothing.

Chad smoothed away her panty hose, opened her jacket and her blouse and pressed his mouth against her breasts. She couldn't stop herself from stroking his back and tight buttocks and unbuckling his belt to free him from his slacks.

What harm could there be in doing, one more time, what they'd already done? Especially when she wanted him so much.

"We need to take precautions," she whispered.

He grabbed a small packet from the bedside table. Jill was too impressed by his dexterity even to consider objecting as he managed to unroll the thing and slip it into place while running his tongue over her breasts.

"You're a man of many talents," she gasped.

"This is my favorite," he murmured, stroking her legs apart. "You have no idea how much I've missed you."

And then, magically, he was inside her. The pleasure was so intense that Jill could think of nothing else, only the searing thrill of his hard shaft and the rioting demands of her own body.

He rolled her on top, and she groaned at the intensity of his deep thrusting. Gripping his forearms for balance, she rode him until she could hardly bear it, and, when the climax came, their cries blended into a sublime counterpoint.

The tension of the past week poured out of her in blissful release. Jill shuddered, grateful for this moment, no matter what might follow.

"That," Chad said, easing her down beside him, "was definitely worth the wait."

She lay against him, treasuring his warmth. "I didn't mean to do this."

"You're a stubborn woman, Jill Rutledge," he said.

"I can see I'm going to have to shower you with presents to get on your good side."

"Please, don't give me the leprechaun," she said.

"Certainly not. I wouldn't dream of letting anyone else torment our favorite twin sisters." Chad's arm kept her pinned against him, but Jill didn't mind. "Now I'll always know which way the wind is blowing. That could be useful."

"Especially if you decide to take your house for a sail," she teased. "By the way, where are what's-their-names? Terror and Blitzkrieg?"

"Torero and Blitz," he corrected. "Vic wanted them back because his father missed them."

"They're Vic's dogs?" Jill asked. "Why didn't you say so?"

"He gave them to me." Chad brushed his cheek against her hair. "Temporarily, as it turned out."

"I thought you were the one who raised two undisciplined animals," she admitted.

"See how you leap to judgment?" His voice vibrated through her. Jill wasn't sure whether she heard the words or felt them. "There's more to me than meets the eye."

"That's for sure." She lay quietly in his arms, until she heard his stomach mutter. "Hungry?"

"The answer to that question is, I have two different appetites, and one of them has been satisfied for the moment," he said. "The other one's starving."

There was nothing in his refrigerator except a hunk of cheese, mayonnaise, pickle relish, some wilted lettuce and a six-pack of beer. "I don't suppose there's such a thing as delivery health food, is there?" he asked.

Jill poked through his pantry. "You've got bean

soup," she announced. "Canned tuna, that's good. Hey, you must have bought this all-natural canned fruit salad by mistake."

"It isn't packed in syrup? You're right," he said from behind her.

When she turned, her arms loaded with cans, she ran right into Chad. He took advantage of the opportunity to plant kisses on her nose and cheeks while she tried to dodge. "Pantry kamikaze," he said. "Better than a video game."

"I hope your microwave works." She ducked under his arm. "Cold soup is the pits."

"I let you get away, you know," he said, following her out.

"The loser has to open all the cans," she replied. "That's you."

They dined on tuna salad, fruit salad and soup. Chad expressed surprise that it actually assuaged his hunger, although he wouldn't give it higher marks than that.

Sitting across from him, wrapped in his spare bathrobe, Jill felt as if the years had rippled backward. For one evening she wasn't a mother or an executive or a divorcée with a past. She was a young woman having fun with a man she cared about.

In his navy robe, Chad radiated masculine contentment. The glimmer of mischief in his smile only made him more appealing.

"I brought a few things back from Colorado." After clearing the dishes, he returned with a gift sack and a small box. "This first one's for Spike, in case he misses the dogs."

Jill peeked into the sack. It contained two small stuffed dogs, a spaniel and an Irish setter, that looked remarkably like Torero and Blitz.

"And this is for you." He handed her a shallow box about the right size to hold a sweater.

"How thoughtful." A bit shyly, she lifted the lid. Whatever he'd picked out, she would wear it, even if it were electric-yellow.

Inside, gift certificates to her favorite health food chain fanned out like the petals of a flower. At its center sat a black velvet jewelry box.

Jill's heart caught in her throat. It couldn't be... No, the box was too large for a ring.

Gently she opened it. Inside, a woven gold necklace nestled against silk fabric. "Oh, Chad!" she breathed. "It's beautiful."

He cleared his throat. "I wanted to buy you a ring to go with it, but I don't know your size. Besides, I figured we should pick it together."

Jill could barely squeeze out the words. "A ring?"

He leaned forward. "I realized that I love you, Jill, and I want to marry you. We haven't known each other very long, but we're old enough to recognize what we want when we find it."

She loved him, too, but his proposal terrified her. It meant she could no longer avoid making the confession that would drive him away.

I can't give you children. I can't be the kind of wife you've dreamed of.

"Marriage may not be what you expect," she began.

"And what do I expect?" He leaned forward, watching her intently.

Children. She tried to say it and couldn't, not so bluntly. "Fun. Games. All your dreams come true."

"Is that what you think of me?" He sat up straighter. "Jill, my thirty-sixth birthday is this Saturday. I'm not an overgrown adolescent, even if I do goof around sometimes.''

Tears burned behind her eyes. She didn't understand why she'd felt so overemotional these past few days, except that she'd missed Chad. ''You didn't let me finish. I was going to say, well, there's a lot we don't know about each other.''

Her comment was meant as a preamble, but he cut off the rest. ''What is it you think you don't know about me? I'll admit it may be a bit childish to paint my living room yellow to annoy the busybodies on the board. But I don't think of life as one big party.''

''I meant there are things you don't know about me.'' The truth hurt so much that she still couldn't blurt it out. She could lead up to it, though, if he'd only listen. ''When I was younger, I couldn't imagine that I would have any limitations. But life didn't turn out to be that simple.''

''Whoa!'' His jaw had gone tight, and the warm glint vanished from his eyes. ''I'm sensing a theme here. Basically that I'm too immature for marriage. Is that right?''

''I didn't mean that you're immature,'' she said. ''Just that you have certain…expectations that I might disappoint.''

''I may not fit everyone's stereotype of 'Father Knows Best,' but that doesn't mean I can't be a good husband,'' he said. ''I guess my playfulness doesn't sit right with you, but it's part of who I am.''

''Chad, that isn't what I meant.'' Jill struggled to find the right approach, but her brain had gone sluggish.

''You don't have to make excuses.'' He scooted his chair away from the table. ''Maybe I am naive. Maybe

I just imagined there was a connection between us, beyond having a good time.''

"I've offended you. I didn't mean to." She twisted her hands in her lap. "I haven't explained things very well."

He responded quickly and definitively. "Let's not keep picking at each other. We both need a few days to think this over. I want you to keep the necklace, in any case."

"I...all right. Thank you." Jill didn't feel right about taking the gift, but to refuse it might anger him further.

Reluctantly she went to get dressed. When she emerged, she saw tension bristling in Chad's shoulders. As she made her way to the door, he averted his gaze.

How had she let matters get into such a tangle? Until now Jill had believed she communicated well, but she'd botched the most important discussion of her life.

"Maybe I should write you a letter about what I meant to say," she told him.

"I can live without any Dear John letters, thank you." His voice was strained.

"I'm sorry," she whispered, and hurried across the back yard and through the gate.

It occurred to Jill as she locked it that without the dogs they could leave the gate wide open if they wished. But there was no longer any reason to.

Chapter Fourteen

On Tuesday before work Chad installed the weather vane on his roof. It might reinforce Jill's impression of his unsuitability, but so what? He wasn't going to change his personality just to disprove a stereotype.

He hammered the nails into place with unnecessary vehemence, all the while wondering why she couldn't see what he was like underneath. Mentally he reviewed his behavior since they'd met.

Okay, so he'd gone off half-cocked lecturing her about responsibility that first day, before he knew the facts about Spike's running away. And his feud with the Norwalk sisters might have gotten a bit out of hand.

But he'd stood up to Aaron that day on the boat, and he'd done everything in his power to rescue Spike from Fiona. Not to mention that he had a highly responsible job that required skill, tact and caring.

If he sometimes acted as though life were meant to be fun and games, there was a reason for it. He'd suffered from burnout before moving to Flora Vista, and he needed to heal. Of course, Jill didn't know about that.

She'd said they didn't know each other very well. In Chad's opinion there was no better time to get acquainted than during an engagement, but, he conceded grudgingly, that might not be reasonable.

He didn't like the notion that he had flown off the handle, but perhaps it was true. Looking back, he could see that Jill hadn't actually rejected him, although he'd assumed that was where she was heading.

At the time it had annoyed him, the way she'd beaten around the bush. He would have preferred that she come right out and tell him she considered him an unworthy lunkhead who was polluting the neighborhood with his presence, if that was so. But he wished now that he'd let her explain herself without interrupting.

Wham! At the burning pain in his finger, Chad jerked back so hard that the ladder teetered away from the roof. He had to perform a virtual high-wire balancing act until it swung forward, coming safely to rest against the house.

"What am I, an acrobat?" he muttered as his finger throbbed. "Darn, that hurts!"

Darn? Had he really said darn? He sounded downright tame!

If he weren't careful, Chad mused, he might forget the string of colorful expletives that he'd collected during his stint in the emergency room. Still, he was glad he hadn't sworn in a voice that might carry all over the neighborhood.

Children might hear him. He especially wanted to set a good example for Spike.

After descending the ladder, Chad put his tools away. The finger still smarted, but he didn't think he'd broken anything.

Gradually he picked up his previous train of thought. Maybe, he mused, he ought to give Jill a second chance to finish whatever she'd been trying to say. He had no intention of allowing her the cowardly escape of writing a letter, but he did owe her a fair hearing.

As he'd suggested last night, they could both use a day or so to cool down. Then he would make his move.

DESPITE HER AGITATION, Jill slept so deeply that she didn't hear the alarm Tuesday morning and awakened with only fifteen minutes to dress for work. Thank goodness she didn't have to get Spike ready, too, since he'd slept over at his friend's house.

That day, in spare moments, she replayed her conversation with Chad and tried to figure out how she should have approached the subject of her inability to have children. She couldn't shout it at him, for heaven's sake!

Judging by his angry reaction, she doubted she'd find another chance to explain. Maybe it was for the best, because in any case she was going to lose him, but she hated to leave him with such a misleading impression.

Chad's playfulness didn't drive her away, it delighted her. It was one of the reasons she knew he'd be a wonderful parent and deserved to have as big a family as he wanted.

Her stomach bothered her until lunchtime, and this time she didn't have Marcia's cookies to blame. Unlike the usual upset tummy, this one demanded to be fed, and she ate more than usual.

On Wednesday and Thursday, she again overslept her alarm, although both times Spike awakened her in time to get ready. Why was she sleeping so deeply? And her insides kept churning with that weird, barfy-but-hungry sensation.

Jill recognized the feeling. She'd experienced these symptoms before—during her ill-fated pregnancy.

She checked her kitchen calendar. It was two and a half weeks since she'd first slept with Chad, and her period was a week overdue.

Was she pregnant? Although she badly wanted to have a baby, her life would be at risk. And she'd be carrying the child of a man she'd antagonized.

There was nothing to be gained by hiding from reality. At lunchtime, Jill drove to a pharmacy and bought a pregnancy test.

DRIVING HOME, Thursday afternoon, Chad slowed when he spotted a small knot of people gathered on the sidewalk a few blocks from home. He recognized association president Sam Wright, Louise and Lorraine Norwalk and a couple of other neighbors.

Louise knelt next to a small, dark shape on the sidewalk. Tears poured down Lorraine's cheeks as Sam talked urgently into his cell phone.

Fear tightened in Chad's chest. Could something have happened to Spike?

As he pulled to the curb, he registered that the crumpled shape was too small and too furry to be a five-year-old. It had to be the Norwalks' miniature poodle.

"What's going on?" he asked as he approached.

Sam clicked off his phone. "I can't believe there's no 911 for animals! Some hit-and-run driver nearly hit the Norwalks. Ran right up on the sidewalk."

"Maxie's bleeding to death." From her kneeling position, Louise regarded him blearily. "Our poor little doggie."

"That teenager just drove off!" sobbed Lorraine.

"I got his license number," said one of the bystanders. "But that isn't going to help Maxie."

"Let me look." Crouching, Chad studied the dog. She was bleeding from several deep cuts in her right foreleg, and a piece of bone jutted through the torn flesh. "It's broken. Let's put on a tourniquet to stop the bleeding."

After receiving a nod, he jogged to his car and retrieved a first-aid kit. With Louise holding the dog, he shut off the bleeding. "I'm no expert on dogs, but I don't see any other life-threatening injuries."

"Can we move her?" Lorraine snuffled.

"She's awake and alert," Chad said. "And wiggling, too. Now that the bleeding's stopped, you should be able to lift her. Don't let her stand on that leg."

"I'll hold her," Louise said.

"We can take my car," said a neighbor. "I live right here."

With everyone pitching in, the dog was soon loaded into the back seat, nestled in Louise's arms. The usually fastidious real estate agent didn't seem to notice the blood and dirt on her clothes.

"Thank you," Lorraine said out the window.

"I hope your dog's all right." With mixed feelings Chad watched them drive off. Who would have believed those two battle-axes could turn so mushy?

He doubted his good deed would make any difference in their dispute. But at least he'd helped an innocent animal.

Heading for home, he drove past Jill's house. In the early dusk, colored lights twinkled along the eaves, and through the front window he could see the merry sparkle of a Christmas tree.

The holiday was less than a week away, Chad realized. He would be working in the morning, and a couple of people at work had suggested he come by for dinner. He'd stalled them, hoping to spend the holiday with Jill.

Maybe he should stop and see her now. Hadn't enough time gone by?

His pager went off. Reluctantly Chad pulled to the curb and dialed the number on his cell phone.

It was the clinic. The doctor replacing him for the evening shift had developed food poisoning. Could he come in for a few more hours?

"I'll be right there," Chad said.

He would have to postpone the visit to Jill.

SHE WAITED until Spike was in bed before using the pregnancy test. *Please don't let it be pink,* she prayed as she waited for the results.

The tube turned a bright rose color. Stunned, she went into her room and sank onto the edge of the bed.

What was she going to do?

In spite of everything, she experienced a thrill to think that life was growing inside her. A baby, Chad's baby. If only she could hold it in her arms, and see the joy on his face as he gazed at it.

But that would never happen. Last time she'd nearly died. And she had not only herself to consider but Spike. He'd lost his parents; he couldn't afford to lose her, too.

Through the rear window Jill stared up the hill toward Chad's house. It was dark except for a security light on the patio. She wondered where he'd gone after work.

It didn't matter. She couldn't turn to him, at least

not until she had more information. He might be a doctor, but that didn't make him a miracle worker.

She needed an obstetrician. The male doctor she'd seen for her last few checkups had been too remote and hurried to entrust with such a delicate situation.

Jill thought of Norma Chen, whom she'd met at Chad's party. An obstetrician, she was pregnant herself. Surely she would help explore all possible options to save both Jill's life and her baby's. She would call first thing in the morning. With luck, when she explained what an emergency this was, the doctor would work her into the schedule.

BECAUSE HE'D STAYED LATE at the clinic, Chad swapped Friday shifts with a colleague and came in after lunch. Otherwise he might never have seen Jill striding toward the ob/gyn building.

He stopped on the walkway, trying to catch her eye, but she didn't see him. In the crisp air her cheeks were a deep pink, a striking contrast to the frosty hair floating behind her.

Even if he'd never seen her before, he would want to know her. As it was, he knew her intimately, and missed her keenly.

"Jill!" At the sound of his voice, she halted. A moment passed before she faced him and, when she did, he saw her lower lip trembling. "What's wrong?"

"N-nothing."

"Oh, yes, it is." Ignoring the curious glances of passersby, Chad hurried to her. From her stiff stance, he could see that he'd guessed right. Something *was* wrong. "What are you doing here?"

"Having a checkup." He heard the fear in her voice.

"Why?" He caught her by the upper arms, determined to find out what was going on. Darn, why had he waited four days before seeing her again?

"I…I might be pregnant," she said.

Until this moment Chad hadn't understood the immense impact such news could have. He heard about pregnancies and saw babies every day. But a child of his own would be miraculous. A dream come true. And yet… "Something went wrong during your last pregnancy. What was it?"

"Not something." Moisture beaded her eyelashes. "*Everything* went wrong. I shouldn't be pregnant. I can't have children."

Suddenly he understood her hesitancy on Monday night, why she'd mentioned limitations and not knowing each other. "Is that what you were trying to tell me?"

Tightly she nodded. "I have to go. I was lucky to get an appointment."

"Who are you seeing?"

"Dr. Chen."

"Good." He trusted Norma. It would help if he could accompany Jill, but he was due at work. "Come and see me when you're done. I'll be in pediatrics." When she hesitated, he added, "Don't you think I have a right to know what she says?"

Reluctantly Jill nodded. "All right."

"Whatever it is, we're in this together," he said.

Norma Chen conducted a gentle but thorough exam and ran another pregnancy test. It confirmed what Jill had found.

"Everything looks fine, but with your history, I want an ultrasound right away," she said. "It's early in the pregnancy, but we can't afford to wait."

"Do you think it could be another ectopic?" Jill's first pregnancy had lodged in one of her fallopian tubes instead of in the uterus. When the fetus grew too large, the tube had ruptured and caused life-threatening bleeding.

"Once you have an ectopic pregnancy, there's an increased risk of another one in the remaining tube." After making a few notes, Norma put the chart aside. She looked at Jill sympathetically. "Under the circumstances I'll make sure the ultrasound technician sees you today."

She noted that, if this pregnancy too were ectopic, she would have to schedule emergency surgery. Then she added something Jill's previous obstetrician hadn't mentioned: that even with both tubes removed, a woman could have a baby with the help of fertility techniques.

Although the information might be comforting to some women, it didn't help Jill. She wanted this baby. She wanted the child that had been planted there when she and Chad made love.

Following instructions, the nurse set up the ultrasound appointment for the earliest time available, two hours from now. It was going to be the longest two hours of Jill's life.

USUALLY ONCE CHAD BEGAN WORK he put everything else out of his mind. Today he had to struggle to focus on each child.

In his spare moments he mulled the stunning news he'd received. Elation mingled with worry and more than a trace of guilt.

No wonder Jill had had trouble explaining the situation on Monday night. He still didn't know the details of what had happened to her, but it must have been devastating.

If only they could have this child together. If only...well, she must be suffering through even more anxiety.

Something darker nagged at him, too, a kind of dread that Chad couldn't put his finger on. It twisted his gut and made him want to deny what was happening. Or to flee from it.

What was going on? He wasn't a coward, and he never ran out on anyone who needed him. Yet he became aware, for the first time, of an abyss inside himself that he wasn't sure he could face.

It involved Jill. And the pregnancy. And the danger.

He had to get a handle on it. He had to root it out. The trouble was, he didn't know where to start.

BY THE TIME JILL RECEIVED the ultrasound photos and consulted with Dr. Chen on how to interpret them, it was almost time to pick up Spike. She'd promised to see Chad, however, so she hurried to pediatrics, where Cynthia ushered her into his private office and went to fetch him.

Clutching the blurry black-and-white images, Jill waited in a padded chair facing the desk. Behind it stood shelves filled with medical texts. On the wall to her left hung diplomas and certificates.

Chad hadn't shown much reaction earlier when she'd told him her news. He hadn't had time to think it over, of course.

When she'd lost her first baby, Gary had acted reassuring at first. They would have another one, he'd said glibly.

Jill wasn't sure when the impact had sunk in back

then, the realization that she'd lost not only that child but any future one. Only then had she seen Gary's true feelings...

"Jill!" Above the white coat, Chad's gray-green eyes gleamed with concern. "Are you okay?"

"I'm...fine." From where she sat, she held out the pictures. "Dr. Chen says the pregnancy appears to be developing normally."

"That's great!"

"I guess so." She couldn't believe it would be that easy. And maybe it wouldn't.

"What went wrong the first time?" he asked, studying the pictures intently.

"My first pregnancy was ectopic." She clasped her hands to steady herself. "It ruptured when I was home alone, and if my mother hadn't stopped by and called the paramedics, I would have died."

"Oh, Jill. I'm sorry." He set the pictures on the desk and crouched in front of her. With his thumb, he wiped a tear from her cheek.

"The doctor said it might happen again and that, since I was also at risk for developing diabetes during a pregnancy, that was two strikes against me. He recommended sterilization," she said.

Chad stared at her, aghast. "Who was this idiot? Just because there's a high risk, that doesn't mean a pregnancy can't be managed."

He sounded like Dr. Chen, which didn't surprise Jill, since she knew they were both fine doctors. But he didn't sound like a man thrilled to learn he was going to be a father. "I know that now."

"This had something to do with breaking up your marriage, didn't it?" he asked.

"Gary took it well at first," she said. "Until it had

time to sink in. Then he decided I wasn't enough of a woman for him.''

"He said that?''

"Yes, when I caught him having an affair with his assistant," she said. "To justify himself, I guess. That was the end of our marriage.''

Chad straightened and leaned against the desk. "I'd say he wasn't enough of a man to stand by his wife.''

"My sentiments exactly." It had taken her years to reach that point, however.

Even now Jill didn't know if another man could accept the risks she ran. The need for close monitoring of her blood-sugar levels. The possibility that any future pregnancy might be ectopic. The reality that she wasn't some glossy, idealized woman from a TV ad.

"You'll be fine, Jill." Chad cupped his hands around hers. "Norma's the best obstetrician I know. And you already live a healthy lifestyle. There shouldn't be any problems." His tone vibrated with sympathy, but that wasn't the same as madly declaring his love. She wanted a man to love her, not another doctor to offer reassurances.

A tap at the door preceded Cynthia's entrance. "Doctor? You've got patients waiting.''

"I'll be right there." When she retreated, he told Jill, "I'm working late tonight, and exhaustion isn't conducive to in-depth discussions. I'll be off at five tomorrow. Can I see you then?''

"Sure. Call me when you get home and I'll make dinner," she said.

He hesitated, then gave her a kiss on the cheek before leaving. She might have been one of his patients, for all the warmth he'd shown.

Shaken, Jill collected the pictures and went to get

Spike. She knew Chad would help her through the pregnancy as a friend.

But the enthusiasm that had spurred him to propose marriage had evaporated. Just as she'd feared.

NERVOUS ENERGY POWERED CHAD through the afternoon. The clinic was so busy he barely had time to run out for a hamburger during his dinner break.

He ought to eat the way Jill did, he reflected as he gobbled down the sandwich. Around him, the fast-food restaurant echoed with voices—a woman at the window taking drive-through orders, a little girl telling her mother about her day, two men discussing the Lakers.

They couldn't drown out the voice inside that called him a coward and a creep. He should have taken Jill into his arms and begged her to marry him. It was what he wanted more than ever, yet...

What if something does go wrong? There could be last-minute complications. What if we plan a future together, and then I lose her?

He didn't understand this excessive worrying. Chad never went around imagining the worst.

One evening in the inner city, he'd confronted a knife-wielding man outside the hospital and delayed him from attacking an ex-girlfriend until the security guards arrived. Chad hadn't been particularly frightened. He'd been buoyed up by the inexplicable certainty that nothing bad was going to happen to him.

Yet, since learning about Jill's situation today, he'd lost his optimism about the future. All he could see ahead were shadowy threats.

Threats that, in some way, revolved around Chad

himself. As if he were the one endangering the woman he loved.

He had to overcome this state of mind, for Jill's sake and for his own. And he had to do it quickly or risk losing what remained of her trust.

Chapter Fifteen

Jill knew Chad wasn't the type to abandon her. But she wanted him to love her beyond any reservations.

In the past weeks she'd come to feel a closeness to him that she'd never felt for Gary, even in their early days. Chad was more than a handsome man and charming companion. He was her friend and soul mate.

Unless she was kidding herself...fantasizing the man she needed and trying to make Chad fit that image.

Despite her relief that the pregnancy was growing in the right place and her mounting excitement about the prospect of having a baby, Jill's spirits remained unsettled. She had trouble falling asleep, although once she did she slept with hormone-induced soundness.

Saturday morning she threw herself into getting Spike ready for the day. Due to the extra pressure of the season, she had to work until three on what would normally be a day off.

Since Yvette had gone to spend the holidays with her son's family and there was no preschool on Saturday, Jill had obtained permission to take her nephew to work with her. The mall had a child-friendly policy, and with only a few days to go until Christmas, what better time to bring a little boy along?

"You're going to help me," she told Spike in the car. "We'll put magazines in the racks, and you can make sure the signs are straight and nothing's falling off the Santa Claus displays."

"You bet!" The boy sat up straighter. "I've been hoping you'd take me to the mall."

"I thought I'd shown it to you!"

"No. You just talk about it a lot."

Although she dropped him off across the street every day, Jill realized with a touch of embarrassment, she'd never taken Spike inside. To her the mall was a place of business rather than an entertainment center.

"We're going to fix that omission today."

"Yeah!" he said, and bounced against his seat belt.

Seeing the mall with a child was a novel experience, Jill soon discovered. Instead of greeting her with comments and gossip, the members of the Dawn Patrol fussed over Spike as if they hadn't seen a little boy in years.

To his delight, they insisted on taking him for a round of exercise while Jill went to check her e-mail. When she collected him, he was beaming.

Although she'd never felt entirely easy about the five Santas, in Spike's company she came to understand their appeal. "It's like I get to be five children who live in different countries!" he told her. "Maybe one of them can give me what I really want."

"I thought you wanted a hand-held video game system and some books and a stuffed bear in a red sweater," said Jill, who'd already bought those toys.

"I do," he said as they walked toward Mrs. Claus's fairy-tale cottage. Two days before Christmas the mall was jammed, and they had to maneuver around milling people. "But what I want even more is for Chad to be my daddy."

Jill's heart squeezed. *That's what I want, too.* "We'll see him tonight," she said. "We're eating dinner together."

"Will there be cake?" Spike asked.

They were passing a maternity shop, and Jill made a mental note that she'd be shopping there soon. "Cake?" she asked. "What happened to ice cream?"

"Oh, ice cream, too!" he said. "After all, it's his birthday."

With everything that had happened, Jill had forgotten the significance of the day. "That's right!"

"He never got birthday parties when he was little," Spike reminded her. "We ought to give him one."

"It's too late to invite his friends."

"We can have a party with three people," her nephew pointed out. "Mom and Dad and I did that last year. We went to the movies and ate supper at Fisherman's Wharf, and then we had chocolates at Ghirardelli Square."

Jill recalled seeing birthday decorations on sale half price at a card shop. Why not throw a little party for Chad? It would break the tension and bring him closer to Spike.

No matter what went wrong between the adults, she didn't want her nephew to lose an important male figure in his life. "Okay," she said. "You can help me plan it."

"Great!" Spike began to skip.

For the rest of the day, in every spare moment, the two of them planned the party. A mall was an ideal place to buy everything except the food.

Marcia insisted on donating a batch of cookies. The

fire inspector, after he finished examining the holiday decorations and the exits, donated three child-size plastic fireman's helmets from a stack he'd brought to give away.

Jill filled two shopping bags with decorations and gifts. She and Spike chose a little stuffed skunk wearing a doctor's coat and stethoscope, the latest Harry Potter book (which they could borrow after Chad read it), a romance novel about a doctor and, at Spike's insistence, a computer mouse pad picturing a cat that looked like Neurotic.

At the supermarket on the way home, they stocked up on birthday cake, ice cream and the ingredients for burritos with whole-wheat tortillas, fresh fruit salad and steamed vegetables. "I have to eat right," Jill said.

"You always eat right," Spike said.

She couldn't tell him about the baby yet. She hadn't even told her mother. Not until she talked to Chad and knew where they stood.

JILL HAD INTENDED to leave a note inviting Chad to her house, where she would stage the party. But when she stopped by his place to leave the message, she couldn't resist checking his doors, and found that the rear sliding one was unlocked.

It would be a lot more fun to surprise him with a party in his own house. Plus, this way he could enjoy the decorations for as long as he wanted.

"I don't think he'd mind if we went in while he's not here," she told Spike. By her watch they had an hour to spare.

After unloading, she drove her car home so he wouldn't see it. She fed the cats, changed into slacks and a sweater and impulsively put on the necklace Chad had given her.

Then she and Spike returned to put up balloons and streamers. As she set the kitchen table with birthday-themed plates and cups, the little boy stuck the candles somewhat crookedly into the cake. He couldn't count to thirty-six so Chad got twenty-two candles instead.

The doorbell rang before Jill could fix the burritos. Fifteen minutes early! She was about to instruct Spike to start singing "Happy Birthday" when it struck her that Chad wouldn't ring his own doorbell.

The bell sounded again, impatiently. It might be the postman with a package, she thought, and went to answer.

It wasn't the postman. It was the Flora Dora Girls, standing on the porch holding a large, gaily wrapped parcel. At their feet sat a miniature poodle with a splint on one leg.

Their eyebrows arched when they saw Jill. Embarrassed, she said, "Chad's still at work. Spike and I sneaked over to throw a surprise party for his birthday."

"It's his birthday?" Louise asked. "How timely."

"We brought him a present," said Lorraine. "He saved our little Maxie's life. Look! She's doing fine now."

Finishing each others' sentences, the two of them told how a hit-and-run driver had injured the dog and Chad had applied a tourniquet. The much-abashed driver, a teenager who lived in the neighborhood, had been caught and had promised to pay all the vet bills from his lawn-mowing money.

"And he's going to cut our lawn free for a year," Louise said.

"It certainly is bright in here." Lorraine peered at the newly painted wall.

"I know he painted it this color to thumb his nose at us, but he's the one who has to live with it," said her sister.

"It isn't really that bad," Lorraine added. "From the inside."

"We'll leave this with you." Louise handed over the parcel. "Hold it flat so it doesn't wrinkle."

From the weight and texture, Jill could guess what it was. "Curtains?"

"They're a lovely shade of cream," Louise said.

"With electric-yellow valances," added Lorraine. "I can't tell you how hard those were to find!"

"I'm sure he'll appreciate them." She was glad to see a truce, although she doubted the war would end so easily.

Maxie whined and poked her nose into Louise's hand. "She's hungry. We have to be getting home."

"Tell the doctor happy birthday for us!"

"I will." Watching the women retreat, with Maxie clutched lovingly in Louise's arms, Jill found herself liking the pair. Well, a little bit, anyway.

Cream curtains might deprive motorists of their colorful view, but it would give Chad more privacy. Chad and anyone else who eventually shared his home.

Determined not to follow that train of thought, Jill went to fix dinner.

MOST OF THE RESIDENTS of the Terrace Crest Estates had decorated for Christmas, Chad noted as he drove home through the early dusk. Red, green, blue and yellow lights twinkled from eaves, white lights dazzled from the branches of low-growing trees, and elves and reindeer pranced on lawns and rooftops.

He wondered if Santas on the roof violated some association ruling. If so, he really ought to get one, but he couldn't work up much enthusiasm.

Chad's usually gleeful attitude had abandoned him. What was wrong with him, anyway? He hadn't figured it out, even though he'd been trying for hours.

As he pressed the garage door opener, he looked through his unshielded front windows and saw a light shining from the kitchen. He must have left it on this morning. If only it meant that someone were home, waiting for him. Other than a burglar, of course.

Inside the garage, silence closed in when he killed the motor. Chad hadn't realized how much he would miss the dogs' eager greeting.

He uncoiled from the sports car, still trying to unsort the tangle in his mind. It was filled with images: of Jill's taut expression yesterday, of Spike trotting alongside him on the sidewalk, of a baby that he couldn't see clearly, lying in Jill's arms. And of his parents' home, filled with books and curios but echoing with their absence.

Stop feeling sorry for yourself. Lots of people get blue during the holidays, with more reason than you have.

Going through the garage, he skirted the all-terrain vehicle he'd bought with fantasies of exploring the desert and hadn't driven since it flipped and tossed him bottom-first into a cactus. He stepped over the lawn mower and narrowly escaped tripping on the skis he'd forgotten to stow overhead. Someone ought to clean up this mess, Chad thought ruefully.

The moment he opened the interior door, he smelled

Mexican food. Someone *had* come to celebrate his birthday.

All of a sudden Chad knew what had been bothering him.

JILL WONDERED what was taking him so long. She'd heard the key scrape and the door open, and knew Chad must have smelled the burritos. Why wasn't he striding in here?

Spike gazed up at her questioningly as they stood in the kitchen, poised to sing birthday greetings. At last the door closed and familiar footsteps approached.

She launched into the song, with Spike joining her. In the doorway, Chad stood watching them with a strange expression on his face, as if he couldn't decide whether to laugh or run away.

It must have been a long day at the clinic, because he looked tired. His hair needed combing, and there was a hollowness around his cheeks.

"Happy birthday!" Jill cried. "I hope you're hungry, because we've got lots of food."

"And the Flora Dora Girls brought you a present," the little boy added. "It's curtains. We got you presents, too."

When Chad didn't answer, she wondered if she'd made a horrible mistake. Maybe he just wanted to be left alone.

Then he smiled. "What an unexpected pleasure. I'm not used to getting gifts. You'll have to show me how to open them, Spike."

"It's easy," the boy said. "Come on." Reaching for a large hand, he led Chad to the side counter where they'd piled the gifts. "First we have to put these on." He handed around the fireman hats.

Chad perched one on his head. "These are jaunty. I guess I missed my true calling. Okay, what's next?"

"Start with this one," Spike said, indicating a package. "It's my favorite."

With the boy's help, Chad unwrapped the stethoscope-draped skunk. "Ah, I think I know him," he said. "This little stinker was in my class at medical school. He was the one whose grades were always better than mine."

"You'd better take a look at this next." Jill handed him the Norwalks' gift.

Chad opened it and studied the curtains with a rueful expression. He read the enclosed card aloud. "'USE THESE.' Is that an implied threat?"

"I refuse to comment."

"I'll put them up one of these days. How's the dog?"

"Maxie's fine." Jill wished she could figure out the reason for his continuing subdued air. In the meantime, she was grateful for any neutral topic.

Chad thanked them for the books and the mouse pad and tucked into the meal with an appetite. Spike filled the silence by chattering about his day at the mall and how much he'd enjoyed meeting the five Santas.

Chad blew out the candles. Whatever he wished for, he kept to himself.

The males enjoyed the cookies, ice cream and chocolate cake. Jill, more determined than ever to keep to her diet, ate a bran muffin.

After dinner Spike yawned several times. "Bedtime," Jill said.

"I could read to him." Chad picked up his new book. "Let's adjourn to your house. Don't worry. I don't mind cleaning up here later."

He seemed pleased with the party, Jill thought. In fact, he frequently paused and gazed around as if savoring the moment.

His glance lingered on her necklace, but he didn't say anything. She supposed it showed discretion, to wait until Spike was asleep before they had their promised discussion, but the suspense was driving her crazy.

What had happened to the outspoken, uncomplicated man she'd come to know over the past few weeks? She didn't want to believe she'd been right, that this pregnancy and its possible dangers had proved too much responsibility for him. Yet it was hard to know what other conclusion to draw.

They trekked through the gate and down to Jill's house. From the slope she could see the blinking lights along the block creating a magical scene.

"Tomorrow's Christmas Eve," she noted, opening her back door.

"Are you doing anything special?" Chad asked.

"I'm not sure." Jill wished she'd planned something in advance, but it hadn't occurred to her.

"Can we go Christmas caroling?" Spike said. "Mom and Dad and I went with their church group last year."

"It's a tradition from my childhood, too. Sounds perfect." She was glad of the suggestion. "Then we'll drink hot chocolate and get warm."

En route to the lamp, Jill sidestepped Normal, who, in a fit of nocturnal activity, had wandered over and was trying to rub her ankles. From the couch Neurotic observed with disdain, being one cat who avoided people's ankles as if they were death traps.

When the lamp came on, Spike scampered off to

brush his teeth. Turning to Jill, Chad asked, "How do you always know exactly what to do?"

"Normal often gets affectionate at night," she said. "I only tripped three or four times before I got the hang of the kitty-sidestep cha-cha."

He grinned. "I didn't mean avoiding the cat. I meant, you didn't blink an eye at Spike's suggestion. Go caroling? Sure thing. And afterward, of course, the only possible thing to do is drink hot chocolate."

"It's obvious." Seeing the warmth in his face, Jill relaxed a little.

"Not to everyone," Chad said. "It's called making a home. Some families never do figure it out."

"Could someone turn on the light in the bathroom?" a little voice called from the hallway. "It's dark in here."

Before he'd finished speaking, Chad hurried to help. As if he were Spike's daddy, Jill thought, and felt a lump form in her throat.

The bedtime ritual was becoming familiar, she noted a few minutes later. She settled into Leah's rocking chair, Spike nestled in the crook of Chad's arm, and the strong male voice rang into her heart as he read the story.

"I'm an orphan like Harry," Spike said after he finished the chapter. "I wish I had magic powers like he does."

"You do," Chad said.

The boy regarded him dubiously. "Oh, yeah? What?"

"You have the power to make people love you," the man said. "And you have a mind capable of imagining happiness. Not everyone can do that."

"That isn't magic," Spike said.

"Oh, yes, it is." Chad gave the boy a light squeeze. "It doesn't violate the laws of nature, so we don't consider it magic. But you and your Aunt Jill have something really special, the power to become a family."

"It only feels like a family when you're here," Spike told him.

Jill was surprised to see a sheen of moisture in the man's eyes. "I'm glad I'm here," Chad said hoarsely.

"You have to come back tomorrow night." When Spike didn't receive an immediate answer, he explained, "To read me the next chapter. You can't start something and not finish it."

"I know." Chad kissed him on the forehead. "Time to hit the hay, buster."

"Okay." Spike pretended to hit the pillow. "Now what?"

"Now you sleep."

Jill came over for her good-night kiss, and the two of them left. She knew from experience that her nephew would fall asleep almost as soon as she turned off the lights.

In the hallway Chad said, "I owe you an explanation."

"For what?"

"The way I've been acting," he said.

Her spirits plummeted. That didn't sound like a preamble to a joyful reconciliation. It sounded like bad news. "All right. Let's go in the living room."

On the couch Jill sat at one end and curled her feet beneath her. Through the thin curtains, she could see blurry colors flashing on the house across the street.

Chad chose an armchair with his back to the window. The twin floor lamps cast interlocking shadows on his face. After the cozy scene in Spike's bedroom, it hurt to see him look so distant.

He propped his long legs on an ottoman. "Ever since you told me you were pregnant, something's been eating at me, but I couldn't figure out what."

The blood thrummed in Jill's veins, and her lungs worked at breathing. Processes that usually happened automatically became an effort, now that she faced the possibility of losing the man she loved.

Loved hopelessly, more than she'd been willing to admit even to herself. Loved more than she'd ever dreamed of loving Gary.

"Tonight, when I opened the door at my house and realized you'd made dinner for my birthday, it was as if I were getting everything I'd ever wanted," he said. "I almost couldn't believe it."

"You don't act very happy about it."

He leaned forward, dropping his feet to the floor and resting his elbows on his knees. "Let me tell you what happened at the hospital where I worked in Los Angeles."

Jill waited, puzzled. What did their relationship have to do with his previous job?

"The place was nothing like the clinic here," he said. "Picture long, bleak corridors, not enough staff, sometimes not enough beds, either. Emergency cases pouring into the emergency room and spilling into the halls."

"Did you deal with emergencies?" she asked.

"Occasionally, when they involved children," he said. "But even in pediatrics, a lot of kids' problems were complicated by poor nutrition and by infections that should have been treated earlier."

Jill shuddered. The scene was a far cry from anything she'd experienced.

"There was a nurse in the E.R. who anchored everyone. Kept us sane," Chad said. "Marie. She was divorced and had three kids, who did their homework in the waiting room, because she didn't like them to go home alone.

"One day I found her crying in the staff room. She tried to hide how upset she was, but I wanted to help."

That sounded like him, Jill thought. She remembered how, that first day when Spike ran off, he'd bought the boy an ice cream cone. And, later, how Chad had intervened with Fiona. "What was wrong?"

"Her abusive ex-husband was in jail, something she never talked about to others. She said that sometimes she got so lonely she almost wished he were back," he said. "I invited her and the kids to a carnival that weekend."

"I hope they had a good time," Jill murmured, her heart going out to Marie.

"We all did. A few weeks later I took them to the county fair," he said. "Over the next year I celebrated birthdays and helped with homework."

"Were you two dating?" She quashed a spurt of jealousy. They were talking about the past, after all.

"Marie and I never went out by ourselves. I don't know if you could say we were involved." In the uneven light she couldn't read his expression. "But she and her kids became a kind of substitute family to me."

"It sounds as if you became their substitute father."

"That's what I thought, too," he said. "Then one day at work, Marie told me her ex-husband had been released on parole. He wanted to make it up to the kids about his absence, and he needed her help to stay away from drugs. So she took him back.''

Jill shook her head at the woman's foolishness. But who was she to judge? Maybe Marie had seen something worth saving in this man. "How did it work out?''

"Fine, for about a month," he said. "Then she turned up at work with bruises on her cheek. She said she'd tripped and hit her face on a door frame.''

"You think he hit her?''

Chad nodded. "I've never been prone to violence, but I wanted to deck the guy. I wanted to teach him what it was like to be used as someone's punching bag.''

"Did she leave him?'' Jill asked.

He stared down at his clenched fists. "No. I guess things got better for a while after that. She said they were in counseling. Two months later he got off parole, and they moved to northern California.''

Across the street, car lights halted at the curb. Jill heard her neighbor's voice call a greeting to someone, but it sounded miles away. "Did you keep in touch?''

"She said not to try to contact her. It made her husband jealous.'' Chad flexed his hands. "After that, life at the hospital became unbearable. I found myself dreading work, lacking energy, not being able to do my best. So I changed jobs.''

"Maybe she tried to contact you and couldn't find you,'' Jill said.

He shook his head. "I sent her my new address in care of the hospital where she was working. She never wrote.''

"It's been over a year, then?''

"Yes. I keep thinking I should have found a way to

get her and the kids out of that situation," he said. "The worst part is I'm afraid her ex-husband found out she'd been seeing someone and maybe that was why he hit her. Instead of helping, I made things worse."

"That wasn't your fault." She ached to touch him, but he was too far away, emotionally as well as physically.

"Then yesterday, when you said you were pregnant, it was as if you had given me the most wonderful gift in the world." Chad gazed at her sadly. "And you did it again today, being there when I got home, making something special of my birthday. It was everything I ever wanted, except..."

She could hardly breathe. "Except what?"

"Except that I could lose you. Lose everything." He glanced toward the Christmas tree. "I read once that when we marry and have children, we give hostages to fate. I never really understood what that meant until yesterday."

Jill struggled to comprehend what he feared and why he had withdrawn. "My pregnancy frightens you?"

"Yeah. Weird, isn't it?" In Chad's lopsided grin, she caught a flash of his familiar boyish side. "The one thing that terrifies me is the prospect of any harm coming to you or the baby or Spike. And I'm the one who put you in this danger, because I got you pregnant."

So that was the problem: he cared too much. How ironic, when Gary had cared too little. The trouble was, Jill realized, that the result might be the same. It would be easier for Chad to bail out now than to make a commitment and have to live with his fears.

"There will always be risks," she said. "Every time

one of us walks out of the house, there's a risk. People who love each other have to be willing to take them.''

"That's what I tell myself," he said. "I keep hoping it will sink in.''

If only he would take her in his arms and tell her he loved her. With a ferocity that startled her, Jill realized that she, too, was terrified of losing what she wanted most.

And there was nothing she could do about it. She had to let Chad work this out in his own heart.

A few minutes later, after making sure Spike was asleep, he kissed her on the cheek and went out. From the patio he said, "What time are you caroling?''

She hadn't given it any thought. "About seven, I guess.''

"I promised to read to Spike at bedtime, so I'll come too, if that's all right.''

"Sure," she said, and watched him disappear into the dimness of the yard.

At least they would spend Christmas Eve together. Right now that was all she could count on.

Chapter Sixteen

On Sunday Chad went to the mall. He'd already bought a model airplane to give Spike on Christmas, but he intended to get the boy a warm scarf to wear tonight. For Jill he wanted an arrangement of dried fruit, since she couldn't eat most desserts.

Mostly, though, he hadn't come to buy things but to absorb the air of gaiety. And to see the scenes that Jill had described, so he would feel more a part of her daily work.

"Care for a cookie?" As he neared the fairy-tale house, Mrs. Claus approached with a plate of chocolate-chip treats.

"Thanks." He tried one. "These are great. Your own recipe?"

She nodded. "Shopping for your wife?"

"Not married," he said between bites.

"Steady girlfriend?"

"Mmm, hmm," he replied.

"Good," she said.

"Why do you say that?"

Mrs. Claus—her name was Marcia, he recalled—studied him with a twinkle in her eye. "Because you look like a lost little boy, and yet you're a handsome grown-up man. I'd say you need someone to take care of you, and someone you can take care of."

"What are you doing tonight?" he asked impulsively. "And don't tell me you're flying around behind a reindeer. I'm old enough to know better."

"Actually, nothing," she admitted. "My daughter and grandkids went to spend the holidays with her husband's family in Minnesota."

"Be at Jill Rutledge's house at 7 p.m.," he said, and gave her the address. "We're going caroling."

"You must be Chad!"

"She told you about me?" he asked, pleased in spite of himself.

"Spike did," she said. "I'll be there."

He wandered by the Christmas-in-Mexico display and, when the line of children dwindled, chatted with Santa José. The man good-naturedly agreed to bring his wife and join them in caroling, too.

Santa Whitefeather, also short of kids at this eleventh hour, was discussing the merits of solar-powered cars with a couple of relatives in Native American dress. They, too, said they'd come.

Making a mental note to buy extra hot chocolate and some marshmallows, Chad made the rounds of the other three Santas. Santa Rafe was eager to bring his wife and daughter, since they were new in town and didn't know many people. Santa Wong, whose family didn't celebrate on Christmas Eve, said he would enjoy experiencing Jill's customs.

The lone holdout was Santa Bob. "I'd love to, but I've been hired for two parties tonight, back to back. It's how I supplement my income."

"If you can sneak away for a few minutes, we'd love to have you," Chad told him. "I understand you're the veteran Santa around here, so your presence means a lot.''

"I'll take down the address, but I doubt I can make it," the man said. "Say ho-ho-ho to Jill for me, will you?"

"Glad to."

By the time he finished his shopping, Chad was whistling "Joy to the World" along with the recorded music. As he stepped into the crisp afternoon air and headed for his car, he realized that his spirits had lifted.

He had no idea why, or how long the mood would last. But he intended to enjoy it while it did.

THAT AFTERNOON Jill called her mother and invited her to dinner. "I know it isn't what we usually do, but if you don't have other plans, we'd love you to join us."

"A couple of friends and I were planning to go out, but both of them had relatives show up unexpectedly," she said. "I was just trying to figure out some way to make myself useful."

"A grandmother is always useful to her grandchild," Jill said. "And her daughter."

"What about…" Nita hesitated, being diplomatic.

"Chad? He's going to join us later for caroling," she said. "I found the lyrics to our favorite carols in one of my scrapbooks. I'll run off extra copies. Some of the neighbors may want to join in when they hear us singing."

"Or they may head for the hills," her mother said.

"I'll take a few pairs of ear plugs, just in case," Jill joked. Then she took a deep breath. "There's something else—well, maybe I should tell you later tonight."

"Tell me now," Nita said. "I hate suspense."

"I'm pregnant." Before her mother could start worrying, she added, "I had an ultrasound. It's fine."

"How does Chad feel?"

"Happy. Confused." She didn't want to go into details. "We haven't made any decisions."

She knew her mother well enough to hear the unspoken lecture, that women were supposed to wait until they'd walked down the aisle before they had children. Jill agreed. On the other hand, she might never walk down the aisle again and, while she wouldn't deliberately choose to have a child alone, she couldn't regret it.

"You know what I think on the subject," Nita said. "Nevertheless, to have another grandchild, well, it's a blessing. I hope everything works out for you, darling. You can count on me."

"I know that," Jill said. "You've always been there when I needed you. I love you, Mom."

"I love you, too," Nita said. "I'll see you in, say, an hour?"

"Perfect."

JILL BAKED oatmeal-raisin cookies. "That's so we'll have some to leave for Santa," she told Spike.

She intended to follow Ellery and Leah's customs as closely as possible. They'd left cookies and milk for Santa, then put the presents under the tree after their son went to sleep.

"I don't think Santa's coming this year," the boy told her sadly.

"Why do you say that?" She stirred the lentil stew she was making for dinner.

"He won't know where to find me," Spike said.

"Of course he will!" Jill told him. "Santa always knows."

"Matt says there's no Santa, anyway." He stole a low-fat corn chip from the package on the table.

Jill made a mental note to have a talk with Matt's mother about what her son was telling other children. "What makes him the big expert?"

"Nothing, I guess. Is Chad coming?" Spike asked.

"He'll be here after dinner," she said. "And I told you, Grandma's joining us."

He brightened. "I'll go watch out the front window for her."

Neurotic wandered into the kitchen and crunched a few mouthfuls of food from his bowl. Jill planned to give the cats canned salmon on Christmas, and she'd bought them each a toy mouse.

What would next Christmas be like? she wondered. The baby was due in late August, so he or she would be four months old.

She pictured a bright-eyed infant lying in Nita's arms, watching Spike unwrap presents. Then she imagined Chad kneeling beneath the tree, assembling a model train set.

Don't ask for too much, Jill told herself.

CHAD ARRIVED half an hour early, while Jill, Nita and Spike were still eating. She invited him to join them, but he'd already dined on take-out. "Fried chicken, my favorite."

"You are joining us for dinner at my house tomorrow night, aren't you?" Nita demanded.

Jill held her breath. To his credit, Chad didn't reveal that she'd neglected to invite him. "I wouldn't miss it for the world." He set a paper shopping bag on the counter.

"What's in there?" Spike asked.

"A few things for under the tree." He removed wrapped packages and set them aside. "And some extra hot chocolate and marshmallows for tonight."

"I've got plenty," Jill said.

"I get real thirsty," he answered, lifting out a large can of cocoa mix and a bag of miniature mallows.

Chad hummed to himself, reinforcing her impression that he had a secret. And a cheerful one, judging by the grins that kept slipping into place before he suppressed them.

Thank goodness he was in an upbeat mood. She didn't dare read too much into it, but it gave her hope. At least they could remain friends. She needed to have him nearby, even if he'd changed his mind about wanting to be her husband.

By seven they'd cleared the dishes and put on their coats. Jill distributed the lyrics to their favorite Christmas songs.

Spike took his solemnly, even though he couldn't read them. Maybe he could pick out a few words, though.

"Were you really planning to go caroling with just two or three of you?" Chad asked as he helped Spike into his jacket and wrapped a new plaid scarf around the boy's neck.

"I figured people would join us," she said. "Or we'd meet up with other neighbors caroling. It's a popular activity in Terrace Crest. Where'd that scarf come from?"

"I bought it at the mall today," he said.

"Thank you!" After a split second, she added, "You went to the mall?"

"Is there some reason why he shouldn't?" Nita interjected. "You don't own it, you know."

"Well, no. It's just that…" The doorbell rang. Puzzled, Jill went to answer it.

Santa Wong stood on the porch in costume, holding a bottle of wine. "Is this the right thing to bring?" he asked. "Everyone talks about holiday spirits."

"It's perfect." Jill ushered him inside and shot a questioning look at Chad. "I take it you two met today?"

"Oh, yes!" said Santa Wong. "You know, it was strange to be Santa and not have anything to do on Christmas Eve. Thank you for inviting me."

"My pleasure." Chad was introducing him to Nita and Spike when the bell rang again.

"I think I sense a pattern," Jill said, and went to let in Santa José and his wife. Marcia was coming up the walk behind them, dressed as Mrs. Claus and carrying a large cookie tin. "Merry Christmas, everybody."

They were joined by Santa Whitefeather and half a dozen of his relatives. Spike bounced with excitement at meeting the two Whitefeather grandchildren, who were a few years older than he.

"You said Santa would come and you were right, Aunt Jill! Not just one Santa but lots of them," he crowed. "Wait till I tell Matt."

Santa and Mrs. Rafe arrived next, with their inquisitive four-year-old daughter, Lilia. "Everyone's here," Chad said after introductions were made.

"Bob's not coming?" Jill asked.

"He's working private parties."

Nita returned from Jill's room with more pages of

song lyrics. She'd given her daughter a fax/copier for her birthday the previous year, and it was doing a yeoman's job tonight.

Ready for action, the group moved outside. In the twinkling of many-hued roof lights, the street took on a carnival air.

"Let's head right," Chad said. "There's more decorations that way." Jill was grateful for the way he took charge, his tall presence and forceful voice helping shape the group into a cohesive unit.

At the first lit house, they launched into "God Rest Ye, Merry Gentlemen." By the time they finished, the residents stood on the porch, applauding.

Down the block they went, working their way through "Deck the Halls" and "Good King Wenceslas." As she'd predicted, others joined them for at least a short distance.

Children's faces appeared in the windows. She could hear them shout, "Mommy! Daddy! Look at all the Santa Clauses!"

"I like this tradition," said Santa Wong.

"I don't know when I've had this much fun," Nita added, her eyes glowing.

"We should do this every year," said Santa Rafe.

"Hey," called one neighbor jovially, "if you guys are here on Christmas Eve, who's delivering the presents?"

"That's Santa Bob," Chad called back. "He had to work tonight, so he gave the rest of us the evening off."

"It's too bad," Jill admitted. "He'd have enjoyed this."

"I'll tell him all about it," Marcia said. "And he'd better plan to join us next year."

"Together forever," said Santa Rafe, who, Jill had learned, was a teacher at a year-round school that gave him December off. "I never thought I'd get sentimental about working this job, but I'm looking forward to it."

The mall's corporate owners had indicated they wanted to hire the five Santas again next year. They were even thinking of expanding the idea to their other malls.

At last the group came to the corner house that belonged to the Norwalk sisters. A thin strand of colored bulbs decorated the porch, and a Christmas tree shone in the window.

A rousing round of caroling brought yapping noises from within. Maxie, who must have been standing on the couch, pushed aside the curtains and pressed her nose to the glass.

The front door opened, and out came the Norwalk sisters, bundled into warm coats. "Wait for us!" called Louise. "We want to sing, too."

"Have some lyrics." Nita handed them sheets.

"Next block, let's start with 'White Christmas,'" Chad called from the front of the procession.

The sisters fell into place, with Lorraine walking alongside Jill. "That doctor's not bad, when you get to know him."

"I'm glad you joined us," she said.

Louise, a few paces ahead, turned and smiled. "Don't think we don't know that you call us the Flora Dora Girls."

"The truth is, we don't mind," said her sister.

"We kind of like the name," Louise said. "Merry Christmas."

Half an hour later the group had grown to two dozen

and had covered four blocks. Some of the children were sagging, and the voices sounded ragged.

Chad lifted a weary but happy Spike onto his shoulders. "Maybe I should run home and get my car so these kids don't have to walk back."

"I don't think that's necessary." Santa Rafe pointed down the street. "It looks like our team has arrived."

Heading toward them was a string of wooden cut-out reindeer, jutting from the front of a minibus. Fitted with sled-type runners on the sides and piled with boxes painted to resemble presents, the bus blasted its horn to the tune of "Jingle Bells."

"It's Santa Bob. Glad he made it," said Santa Whitefeather.

"Ho-ho-ho!" came an answering cry, and the sled-like bus halted. "Anybody need a ride?"

The children were hoisted inside along with a few adults, and the others trouped back on foot to Jill's house. Chad, Marcia and several of the Santas' wives kept busy making hot chocolate and distributing cookies and marshmallows.

More neighbors came to greet the five Santas, and soon the entire block was having a party. Although the residents had always been friendly, Jill had never seen them quite this cozy.

"You're good for Terrace Crest," she told Chad as he handed out plastic foam cups of hot chocolate.

"Agreed," said Louise.

"Does this mean I can paint my house any color I want?"

"No," said Lorraine.

"I didn't think so." He chuckled. "Thanks for the curtains. I plan to put them up next week. It has been a bit awkward when I forget and walk through the living room in my bathrobe. Or less.''

"We especially like the striped pajamas," said Louise.

Even in the diffused lighting, Jill could see that Chad was blushing. "I'm putting the curtains up tomorrow morning. First thing."

By nine-thirty the group dispersed. Marcia stayed to throw the cups into the recycle bin and to chat with Nita. Jill was pleased to hear Mrs. Claus accepting an invitation to join them for dinner on Christmas.

At last only she, Chad and a very sleepy Spike were left. He fell asleep halfway through the second chapter of the book.

"Thank you," Jill said as they tiptoed out. "You made tonight very special."

"It isn't over yet," Chad said. "I gather it's your family tradition to open gifts on Christmas morning, but there's one you should check out tonight."

Jill had seen him unloading several parcels when he arrived, but the one he plucked from his pocket was much smaller. It was a red velvet jewelry box.

Gingerly she accepted it. He'd said last Monday that he didn't want to pick a ring because they should choose it together, so perhaps it was earrings to go with her necklace.

Jill held the velvet box in her hand. She was afraid to open it.

"I don't want to rush you," Chad murmured close to her ear, "but I'm a little tense here."

"Sorry." When she lifted the lid, the light from the tree bulbs caught the sparkle of the diamond ring. Quietly Chad said, "I was hoping for a short engagement. What do you think?"

IT OCCURRED TO HIM that the remark might sound a bit flippant. He'd already proposed once, though. It might bore her if he repeated himself.

On the other hand, maybe not. "Remember that part about I love you and I want to marry you? Well, it still stands."

Jill lifted the ring from the box and slid it onto her finger. He took that as a good sign, even though it was a little loose.

"Perfect," she said.

"We can have the jeweler size it," he offered.

"No, my finger's going to swell while I'm pregnant." She started to laugh. "Listen to me! I must be the most unromantic woman on earth."

"Why do you say that?" He'd thought she was doing rather well.

"The answer is, I love you, too, and what took you so long?" she said.

This conversation, he realized, was entirely too vertical. "We should be sitting down. Preferably with you on my lap."

"That can be arranged," she said.

He eased onto the couch and gathered Jill in his arms. She smelled like hot chocolate and pine needles. With her frosty hair and delicate features, she reminded him of an angel.

Her nose grazed his neck as she snuggled against him. Chad didn't want to think or talk anymore, just kiss her, but he did owe her an explanation.

"Remember what I said about being afraid of losing the people I love most?" he murmured.

"I remember."

"I've always taken charge of my life." He tucked a strand of hair behind her ear, not because it needed to be there but because he liked to fuss over her. "I can't bear to let things get out of hand. That's why I felt so cut adrift, because for once there was nothing I could do to protect you or Spike or the baby."

"What changed?" she asked.

"My attitude." Chad tried to figure out when the shift had occurred. It had been today, he realized, at the mall. "I started to focus on the precious moments I want to spend with you. It finally hit home that taking control of our lives is basically an illusion. All we have is the present."

"One day at a time," Jill murmured, resting her head on his shoulder.

"I knew that intellectually," he said. "Now I know it in my heart."

She tilted her face and kissed him. "Then let's make the most of it."

That sounded like a grand idea to Chad.

Epilogue

"…seven, eight, nine, ten." Spike wiggled his fingers. "If I'm going to count higher, I have to take off my shoes."

"Not in the elevator, please," Chad said as they stopped at the hospital's third floor. "We'll have people dropping like flies."

The little boy giggled. "Anyway, Mrs. Sanchez says I'll do fine in kindergarten," he told Chad as they started down the hall. "She says I'm ready."

"You're a smart kid. If it weren't for you, I'd never have kept track of who likes pepperoni and who likes cheese."

Although Spike's September birthday was still two weeks away, they'd celebrated early so his preschool friends could attend. The previous week Jill and Chad had shepherded ten youngsters to a movie and out for pizza.

"Dad?" Spike had begun calling Chad by that endearment since the wedding six months ago.

"What is it, little guy?"

"I know Leah's birthday is close to mine. Does that mean we have to share a party from now on?"

Chad drew the boy to one side of the corridor and

crouched to his level. "I spent my whole life not getting a real birthday party. Do you think I'd do that to my own son?"

"I guess not, huh?" said Spike.

"Absolutely not." He hugged the boy. "You know, having a little sister may be inconvenient at times, but it'll be fun as she gets older."

"Oh?" The kid had perfected a skeptical lift of the eyebrow, and he wasn't even six yet.

"There'll be more toys in the house, for one thing." Chad stood, and they resumed their journey toward the maternity ward. "And you get to eat cake and ice cream at her birthday party as well as yours."

"Cool!" Spike said. "The thing I like about her is that she's kind of cute. But is she my sister or my cousin?"

Jill's adoption of her nephew had gone through soon after the marriage, and Chad's would be complete in the fall. "Your sister," he said. "And your cousin. Two for the price of one."

"Good deal," the boy said, and skipped ahead down the hall.

THE MATERNITY PANTS were baggy, now that she'd delivered the baby, but not as baggy as Jill would have liked. She couldn't wait to get fit again. It should help that she planned to take Leah for long walks in the stroller.

After snapping on her new nursing top, she brushed her hair in the bathroom and went back into the hospital room to gaze again at her beautiful, perfect baby. She couldn't believe they were going home today and that she'd have this little doll to herself.

The mall had granted a three-month leave of absence. Nita, who was retiring from her job, had decided to move closer, so she'd be watching her granddaughter during the day, after that.

Although she would miss spending long hours with Leah, Jill was looking forward to being at the mall during the upcoming Christmas season. She loved the excitement and had helped design improved settings for the five Santas and Mrs. Claus.

There'd be lots of presents under the Markham tree, too. Jill intended to enjoy every minute of the shopping.

"Hi, Mom!" Spike popped into the room.

"Good to see you in clothes again!" Chad gave her a quick hug, then went to the crib. "How's my little girl? Wide awake, I see." He grew more handsome every time she looked at him, Jill thought with a mixture of awe and unease.

He'd been wonderfully supportive during her pregnancy. But now, with some weight still to lose, she felt clunky and not quite her old self. Plus breast-feeding was new to her, and she hadn't slept well last night from the excitement. How did she look to him?

"Did the other baby go home?" Spike indicated the empty second bed in the room.

"Mom and son left an hour ago." Jill ruffled his hair. "The nurse went to get my release forms."

"Can I watch TV?"

"Sure."

He clicked on the set and was soon absorbed in a cartoon. Jill sat on the bed. Her muscles ached from eight hours of labor the night before last.

Like all high-risk pregnancies, this one had involved a lot of uncomfortable tests and frequent doctor visits.

However, there'd been no complications, and the baby was in excellent shape.

Chad sat beside her and plucked a folded sheet of paper from his pocket. "I wanted you to see this. It arrived at the clinic today."

It was from Marie, his nurse friend, Jill saw. She wrote that she'd left her ex-husband when she realized his occasional temper tantrums were becoming a cycle of abuse.

"If it weren't for you, I might not know what it means to have a man treat me right," she wrote. "The kids and I will be living with my parents in Pennsylvania. I want them to grow up experiencing the way a family ought to be. Thanks for caring."

"That must make you feel good." She handed it back to him.

"It's a relief. I was worried about her. I'm a little concerned about you, though." Chad's gray-green eyes surveyed Jill tenderly. "Your mouth is drooping at the corners. Since I'm such a caring guy, I insist you tell me what's wrong."

"It's nothing," she said. "Postpartum blues, I guess. I feel chubby and a little...insecure."

"About what?"

"How I look. How you feel about me. It's silly, I know."

"No, it isn't silly." Chad picked up her right hand and tapped each finger for emphasis. "Let me count out the answers to your questions."

"I get five answers?" she said.

"Yes, and I'll use the other hand if I need to," he teased. "You'd better hope I don't have to take your shoes off to count higher, the way Spike does."

"Heaven help us," she said.

"One, in case you were wondering, I would have married you even if we could never have a child," he said. "Two, we can have another one or not, or we can adopt another one if you want. Or we could get two large dogs."

"Forget the dogs," she said.

"Three, you don't look fat, you look like a healthy new mom," he said. "Four, your breasts are absolutely gorgeous and I hope you breast-feed for at least three years."

"Don't count on it," said Jill.

"And five, did I tell you the Flora Dora Girls found a renter for my house?" He'd moved in with Jill after the wedding. "They're ready to sign a year's lease."

"Do you have to repaint?" she asked.

His face lit up with mischief. "They love the yellow living room. They said it was one of the main attractions."

"You're kidding!"

"You should have seen Louise's expression when she told me last night," he said. "It was priceless."

The nurse returned with the release papers, and a volunteer came to wheel out the baby's crib, according to hospital policy. Spike clicked off the TV. "Make sure my sister's warm enough," he told the volunteer.

"It's August," the woman said. "And she's got pajama feet on her cute little outfit."

"Well, we don't want her to catch a chill." Jill had never seen her nephew display such grown-up concern.

"I'll tuck a blanket around her," she promised, digging into the diaper bag for one. "Why are you so worried?"

"He came to an important decision last night," Chad told her. "About his future."

"His future?" She wasn't sure she could deal with a cosmic plan laid by an almost-six-year-old. "What decision?"

"I decided what I'm going to be when I grow up," Spike replied as she bundled a receiving blanket around Leah.

"What do you want to be?" asked the volunteer.

"A doctor, like my dad."

"You'll have to work very hard." Jill collected her belongings.

"Years and years of medical school," warned the nurse.

"But I'll get to take care of people, and that makes them love you," Spike said, thrusting his small hand into Chad's big one. "And that's not all."

Jill and Chad exchanged glances. "Ice cream," they both said.

"Yeah. I'm giving out ice cream bars to all my patients," the boy said, and tugged his father toward the door. Then he stopped and looked at Jill. "Nonfat," he added.

"The kid's a fast learner," Chad said.

"I'm hungry." Since her milk came in last night, she'd been ravenous. "Could we stop somewhere for a snack on the way home?"

"Sure," Spike answered as if he were an adult. "I know just the place."

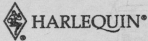
HARLEQUIN®

makes any time special—online...

your romantic escapes

━Indulgences━━━━━━━

♥ Monthly guides to indulging yourself, such as:
  ★ **Tub Time:** A guide for bathing beauties
  ★ **Magic Massages:** A treat for tired feet

━Horoscopes━━━━━

♥ **Find your daily Passionscope, weekly Lovescopes and Erotiscopes**

♥ **Try our compatibility game**

━Reel Love━━━━━━

♥ **Read all the latest romantic movie reviews**

━Royal Romance━━━

♥ **Get the latest scoop on your favorite royal romances**

━Romantic Travel━━

♥ **For the most romantic destinations, hotels and travel activities**

HINTE1

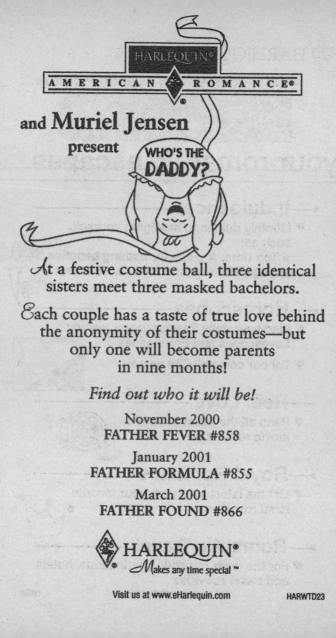

Tyler Brides

It happened one weekend...

Quinn and Molly Spencer are delighted to accept three
bookings for their newly opened B&B, Breakfast Inn Bed,
located in America's favorite hometown, Tyler, Wisconsin.

But Gina Santori is anything but thrilled to discover her
best friend has tricked her into sharing a room with
the man who broke her heart eight years ago....

And Delia Mayhew can hardly believe that she's
gotten herself locked in the Breakfast Inn Bed
basement with the sexiest man in America.

Then there's Rebecca Salter. She's turned up at the
Inn in her wedding gown. Minus her groom.

*Come home to Tyler for three delightful novellas
by three of your favorite authors: Kristine Rolofson,
Heather MacAllister and Jacqueline Diamond.*

HARLEQUIN®
Makes any time special ™

Visit us at www.eHarlequin.com

PHTB